Lands of Our Ancestors
Book One

Gary Robinson

ISBN 978-0-692-78018-3

Dedications

1. This work is dedicated to the loved ones in my life: my kids, Anisa and Rain, who make me proud; my perfect life-mate, Lola, who inspires me, grounds me and helps make it possible for me to create; my father, who has been an anchor and example all my life; and my mother, who waits on the other side.

2. It is also dedicated to future generations of Indigenous People. May we never forget who we are or where we come from. And may we always remember our ancestors, the sacrifices they made and the traditions they fought so hard to keep.

Acknowledgments

I'd like to thank the following people for their valuable input on the Chumash cultural and linguistic aspects of this story: 1) Nakia Zavalla, a descendant of the Santa Ynez Band of Chumash Indians, Cultural Director and a state-certified teacher of the Samala Chumash language, and 2) Chumash tribal member Kathleen Marshall who is also a member of the California State Oversight Committee on Indian Education and a state-certified teacher of the Samala Chumash language.

I'd also like to thank fourth grade teacher Dessa Drake of Templeton, California, for her feedback on the educational value of this book. She tested the book with her class and gathered valuable information on its effectiveness as a teaching tool for the "Mission Unit," which is taught every year in California schools.

I greatly appreciate all their contributions to this work.

It would be a mistake to not also acknowledge the debt we all owe to J.P. Harrington and the tribal consultants he interviewed in the early years of the 1900s. Knowledgeable Chumash people shared their wisdom and teachings with him, and those words are what have helped to connect contemporary California Natives with their own pasts. Maria Solares and Fernando Librado are among those valued Chumash tribal ancestors who worked with Harrington.

Note to Teachers and Parents

This work of historical fiction depicts what might have happened when a village of Chumash Indian people encountered the Spanish padres and soldiers who came to California to establish religious missions and create colonial outposts in the area. The missions, presidios and settlements they established all relied on forced Indian labor to operate, a fact that has been hidden from public view far too long.

Spanish colonial Franciscan priests, led by Junipero Serra, ultimately forced Indians to build twenty-one of these institutions between San Diego and Sonoma, impacting the lives of at least 100,000 indigenous people from forty or more different tribes.

What happens to the Chumash characters in Lands of our Ancestors is typical of what may have happened to all the tribal people who came into contact with any of the missions built on their ancestral lands. That being said, we must also recognize that the experiences of "missionized" Indians were diverse and varied so no one story can cover the full range of possibilities.

The Native American people known as Chumash have lived in the same south-central region of California for at least thirteen thousand years. Made up of separate, small, self-governing groups spread over several thousand square miles, these communities spoke different Chumash languages.

The tribal group portrayed in this book lived (and continue to live) in the Santa Ynez Valley and spoke (and are learning to speak again) one of the Chumash languages called "Samala."

In many history and archaeology books,

their language is called "Ineseño" because these Indian people became associated with the Santa Inez Mission (*Santa Ines* in the original Spanish). Other groups of Chumash are known as Barbareño and Ventureño because they became known as the Indians living in or near those missions (Santa Barbara and Ventura).

In this book, when the Chumash language spoken by the main characters is mentioned, I am referring specifically to the Samala Chumash language spoken by the people of the Santa Ynez Valley. However, to simplify the telling of the story, I have simply referred to it as the Chumash language.

So you can understand what the main characters are saying, you will read most of their words in English. Later in the book, as the Chumash people are forced to learn the Spanish language, you'll continue to understand what they are saying by reading their words in English.

The following is a guide to the Samala Chumash words used as character names in this story, along with their meanings:

Kilik (<u>Kee</u>-leek) - Sparrow Hawk

Tuhuy (Too-<u>hooy</u>) - Rain

Salapay (<u>Sal</u>-uh-pie) - To lift or raise up

Solomol (<u>Soh</u>-loh-mole) - To straighten an arrow

Wonono (Wo-<u>no</u>-no) - Small owl

Yol (rhymes with pole) - Bluebird

Stuk (Stuke-rhymes with Luke) - Ladybug

Kimi (Kee-mee) - To repeat or do over

These Chumash words, as well as many of the book's English words, are part of the "Words to Know" section of the valuable <u>Teacher's Guide</u> that is available to educators to accompany this book. The guide contains many important elements that will help teachers use <u>Lands of our Ancestors</u> as an alternative resource and help students understand this topic within the context of the 4th grade Mission Unit.

x

Table of Contents

Introduction

This is a work of historical fiction based on historical facts. The characters are made up, but through them you will be able to learn what happened to the real Native Americans when Spanish priests and soldiers arrived in California and began building missions, presidios (military forts) and settlements in the region in the 1700s. You will also be able to learn more facts about this period of history by reading any of the books listed in the bibliography at the back of this book.

As you read this story, ask yourself these questions. What would you do if strange men with powerful weapons, and animals you'd never seen before, moved into your homelands and began taking control of everyone and everything you knew?

What if they tricked you into believing they were there to help you when they really had completely different intentions. Those are the questions Kilik (this story's main character) had to ask himself when these things happened to him.

Chapter 1 - Preparations

"Roll the hoop faster this time," twelve-year-old Kilik called out to his cousin. "I have to prove to Father that I'm ready for our overnight hunting trip."

His cousin, Tuhuy, returned to the starting point ready to roll the hoop once more. The boys were playing one of their favorite games of skill: hoop-and-pole. One boy would roll the small hoop on the ground while the other one threw a long, spear-like pole at it. The goal of the game was to send the pole through the hoop.

But to the boys, this was more than a mere game. It was part of their preparation to become men. It helped them to become skillful hunters, and Chumash youth had been rolling the hoop and throwing the pole for countless generations.

"You're already a better shot than any other boy in the village," Tuhuy said. "I'm sure you'll do fine on the hunt." He stood at the edge of their little homemade playing field prepared to spin the hoop again.

"Go!" Kilik yelled, and his younger cousin sent the hoop rolling faster than ever. At just the right moment, Kilik hurled the long, thin pole toward its moving target. And, as before, the spear thrust dead center through the middle of the hoop.

"And another jackrabbit bites the dust!" Tuhuy proclaimed as he retrieved the spear and target again. Carrying the objects back to Kilik, he asked, "Is it my turn yet?"

"Almost," Kilik replied. "But first I need to take a few shots at the hoop with my bow. That's the true test of a hunter's skill."

Eleven-year-old Tuhuy blew out a breath in frustration. He knew he'd never be as good as his cousin at doing anything. But he never ceased trying.

Kilik's name, which meant "sparrow hawk," was well suited to him. He'd always moved with coordination and confidence, achieving things seemingly without much effort.

Tuhuy, on the other hand, found that much physical effort and practice had been required of him. He was more of a thinker. His father had given his name, which meant "rain," because of a dream that foretold of the boy's birth as well as his name. Tuhuy's spirit had reached out from the Spirit World to make his presence known ahead of time.

In spite of their differences, the two boys had been inseparable from an early age. They were like the front and back of the same hand. Or the light and dark that formed one whole day.

Kilik walked to the nearby tree that held his bow and quiver of arrows. Just as he slung the quiver over his shoulder, a man's voice called out from across the creek.

"Kilik! Tuhuy! What are you boys doing?"

The boys turned in the direction of the voice to find Tuhuy's father coming into view.

"Uncle Salapay!" Kilik called out. "Over here!"

As far as Kilik was concerned, his uncle was the ideal Chumash man. He seemed to know everything and could do anything. His muscled brown skin testified to his strength and endurance.

Even his name, Salapay, meaning to raise or lift up, matched what the man was capable of. Although Kilik, of course, loved and admired his own father, his Uncle Salapay was the kind of man Kilik wanted to be.

But at the moment, this ideal Chumash man was angry.

"Don't you see where Grandfather Sun is in the sky?" he asked as he drew nearer. "Can't you tell what time of day it is?"

Both Tuhuy and Kilik looked toward the bright torch in the sky and realized that Grandfather Sun was right overhead. It was mid-day. But, like kids everywhere, Chumash boys weren't known for keeping track of the sun's progress across the sky.

"And where are you supposed to be right now?" Salapay asked.

The boys had to think hard. Tuhuy's eyes brightened as he found the answer to that question in the back of his mind.

But immediately his eyes darkened as he understood what his father was angry about.

"We're supposed to be back in the village helping to prepare for the ceremony," he admitted timidly. "Oops."

"That's right," Salapay affirmed. "Oops. Everyone in the village has a job to do. And everyone must do his job in order for us to be ready for our guests. You know it's one of the most important events of the year."

"But Uncle, I have to get ready for my first hunt with Father," Kilik said. "Bringing back meat is part of my job for this year's festival. But I can't practice my hunting skills without your son's help."

Kilik had almost forgotten what a busy time of year this was. Summer was quickly fading, and Autumn was fast approaching. That meant it was time for the yearly harvest gathering–Hutash.

For the Chumash people, Hutash was both the name of their harvest ceremony and their name for Mother Earth. She provided all things necessary for people to live, and she deserved praise and thanks for it. Chumash people from villages near and far would be attending the gathering, and Kilik's village, the Place of River Turtles, was the host.

Salapay put a hand on his nephew's shoulder.

"I'll tell you what," he said. "You and Tuhuy come back to the village with me now, and I'll help you practice with your bow before dark. How's that?"

"Good," his nephew said excitedly. "Great. Awesome."

Salapay escorted his son and nephew back to the village where everyone was hard at work. The dance arena had to be cleared and smoothed.

Additional housing for visitors had to be added or repaired. Food had to be gathered and stored. It was a lot for the people of the village to accomplish.

Soon the three reached the edge of the Place of River Turtles. Tuhuy and his father headed for their home on the far side of the little town. Kilik walked quickly to his house so he could put away his things.

A large pile of tule reeds lay just outside Kilik's family home waiting to be woven into the reed walls. This was done at least once a year to keep the structure strong and sturdy.

A Chumash house looked a little like half an orange turned upside down. Only it wasn't orange. It was green when the long reeds were fresh, and brown after the reeds dried out. The open doorway faced east to greet the morning sun.

"Your father has been looking for you high and low," Kilik's mother, Wonono, said as he entered their home. "He's expecting you over at the dance arena."

"Sorry, Mother. I got busy practicing for the hunt and let the day slip away from me."

As Kilik put away his bow and quiver, his younger sister bounced in through the open doorway carrying her little doll made of rabbit fur. At six years of age, she thought she was the boss of everyone, especially her older brother.

"Father said you won't be going hunting with him if you don't get to the dance arena immediately," she said. "Immediately!"

"I already got the message, Kimi," her brother said. "You don't have to tell me again and again like you do."

Although she had been named Stuk, which meant ladybug, Kilik preferred the nickname he'd given his sister: Kimi. It meant "to repeat" things, which she did all the time. All the time.

"Stuk, you need to mind your own business and take care of your own ceremony preparation duties," Mother said in a gentle, but firm, tone. "Please get back to the acorn granary so you can help your auntie."

"Yes, ma'am, I'm going," Ladybug said. "I'm going."

She skipped away, turning back to her brother momentarily to give him a scornful look.

When Kilik got to the dance arena, he found his father using a leafy tree branch to smooth out the ground. This area would be used for ceremonial dances during Hutash and needed to be free of rough stones.

"It's good that you finally showed up, son," Kilik's father said in a kind voice. "Our elders and the chief want to see that all of us are doing our part. It shows that the people of this village are strong in our traditions."

Kilik's father, Solomol, had a good position within the village.

He made high quality tools and hunting weapons that everyone wanted. In fact, his arrows and bows were worth more shell bead-money than anyone else's in the region. This was a source of pride for Kilik's family.

Solomol handed his son the branch he'd been using and motioned for Kilik to continue smoothing the soil.

"Kimi–I mean Ladybug–said you weren't going to allow me to go on the hunt if I didn't get over here immediately," the boy said.

"Now does that sound like something your father would say?"

"I guess not. You and Mother are so patient with us."

"I think Stuk has a little of the coyote in her," Father said with a chuckle. "She can be a trickster and a liar, but she never means any real harm. Not like old Coyote in our stories."

"Grandfather told us what we should do whenever we see a coyote," Kilik said as he swept the branch from side to side. "He said to clap our hands three times and chase him away. Maybe that's what I should do to Stuk when she acts like one."

Father and son talked and joked easily as they continued their work.

Kilik missed his grandfather, and the stories he told. That man had learned much from the old ones. And he'd made sure each of his grandchildren heard the teachings and learned the songs and stories that kept the Chumash on the right path of life.

Chapter 2 - House of the Moon

The following morning, Kilik woke up before the sun rose. The big day had finally arrived, and he didn't want to miss a moment of it. A boy's first real hunting trip away from the village was a big deal. If he could bring home meat for Hutash, the village chief would be good to his family. It also meant Kilik would be considered a worthy member of the village.

Solomol and Wonono soon awoke and began preparing for the overnight trip. Solomol gathered the hunting gear they'd take with them.

He also slipped on the talisman necklace he wore on every hunting trip. It was a piece of deer antler attached to a string made of deer hide. The necklace had been blessed by one of the village ceremony leaders, one of the Twelve. It would bring its wearer good luck and help to sharpen his hunting skills.

Kilik's mother packed dried deer meat in a pouch along with other food, and she filled a water basket with fresh water. Soon father and son were off on their great adventure.

"We're headed for some of the best hunting grounds in this valley," Solomol said as they left the village. "I want you to remember how to get there, because some day soon you'll be hunting on your own."

This excited Kilik almost more than he could stand.

"All right, Father," he said. "I'll pay close attention."

The pair first headed north from the Place of River Turtles. The pre-dawn light was just bright enough for them to find their way across the rolling, tree-covered ground. The path first took them up a small hill away from the village and the river. At the hilltop, Solomol stopped.

"Look to the east," he told his son. Kilik cast his gaze in that direction. A low fog hung over the riverbed below them as it did on many mornings. But above the fog layer, the sky was clearer.

"There she is," his father said. "Morning Star wakes up early to light the dawn before Grandfather Sun begins his journey."

Kilik saw the large brilliant star sitting low in the eastern sky just above the horizon.

"At this time of day, the first thing to look for when seeking this trail is Morning Star," Solomol continued. "She rises from the same place every day. Head straight for her and you won't miss the trail."

Then Kilik's father turned back to look down the path they had just walked. Kilik looked down the path as well. Their village, the center of Kilik's world his whole short life, was visible just below them. It sat on a raised, flat piece of ground overlooking a bend in the river. Surrounded by the fog that hovered just over the water, the village appeared to float on clouds.

"I love our village," Kilik told his father. "And I love this valley, the mountains that surround us–our whole Chumash world."

The Chumash world that Kilik loved was an all-natural world. Everything the people ate, used or made came from the rocks, soil, plants, trees and animals around them. They knew this world, and everything in it, very well. They considered it all sacred ground, a gift from Creator.

"Yes, our people have been here for generations," Solomol said. "Our lives are part of this place, and this place is part of us. That's why I want you to never forget who you are and where you come from."

With one last look at the Place of River Turtles, the pair continued on their journey. Grandfather Sun began rising into the sky, carrying his torch in his daily journey from east to west.

Soon their narrow path crossed the valley's main trail running east and west. For who knows how long, humans and animals had used this trail and others to get where they needed to go. The Chumash territory was crisscrossed with well-known trails that led to familiar places.

"We're making good time," Solomol said after awhile.

Just then, the tall grass rustled to their right. A fast-moving jackrabbit burst into view, then froze.

Kilik froze, too. After two quick breaths, the little creature turned and sped off back into the brush.

"I wasn't ready," Kilik complained. "That happened so fast."

"Real rabbits aren't like the hoops in your hoop-and-pole game," Father said. "They don't wait for you to say 'go.'"

Kilik slid his bow from his shoulder where it had been hanging and withdrew an arrow from his quiver. Nocking the arrow, he looked at his father.

"I'll be ready next time," he said.

Solomol smiled and walked on. Unfortunately, they didn't see another rabbit for the rest of the morning.

At mid-day, the trail they were on opened on to a clearing, and in the middle of the clearing stood the largest oak tree Kilik had ever seen.

"She's called Mother Oak," Solomol said.

"As far as we know, she is the oldest oak in the valley. Our people have gathered acorns from her for generations."

As the pair approached the tree, they saw two Native men sitting in the shade eating. Solomol recognized them as friends from a Chumash village further east. He greeted them.

"Haku, friends," he said, using the familiar Chumash word for hello. "What brings you this way?"

"Haku, brother," the older man responded. "Same as you. Hunting food for Hutash."

He pointed to a spot near the tree where a deer carcass lay. The deer's legs were tied to a long pole that the men used to carry the animal.

"I hope you left one for us," Kilik's father said jokingly. "This is my son's first serious hunt."

"Don't worry," the older man said.

"There's plenty more where that came from. It's a good season, so we have a lot to be thankful for."

Kilik and his father sat near the men and opened their lunch pouch. Kilik's feet were beginning to hurt a little from the walk, and he was glad they took a break. The boy listened as the men talked for a short while about hunting, fishing and food gathering. It <u>had</u> been a good year, they agreed.

Soon, both hunting parties finished their small meals and were ready to move on. Before leaving, the older man approached Kilik and Solomol.

"Have you heard about the strange men who have entered our lands?" the older man asked in a serious tone. "They speak an odd language and wear odd clothing that covers their entire bodies."

"Who are they, and where did they come from?" Solomol said.

"No one knows for sure," the man replied. "They traveled first to the lands of our neighbor tribes in the south. And they seem to possess powers beyond anything our own ceremony leaders have ever seen or known."

Kilik spoke for the first time.

"How is that possible?" he asked. "Our ceremony leaders know how to keep the natural and spiritual forces in balance so we can have good lives."

This comment surprised Solomol. He looked at his son with questioning eyes.

"Salapay taught me," Kilik said. "He says its part of his duties as Uncle to teach me about such things."

After a little more conversation, the two parties went their separate ways.

"So at this place we turn and head north," Solomol said to his son.

"I don't see a trail," Kilik said as he scanned the landscape.

His father walked to the north edge of the clearing and pointed with his bow to small break in the grassy underbrush.

"Right here. I call this the Path Made by Deer. It's really an animal trail created by generations of animals who passed through here on their way to a watering hole or feeding grounds."

"The Path Made by Deer," Kilik repeated.

"It's a little hard to find, so remember what this area looks like," his father said. "It will take us to the old hunting camp near the foothills where game is usually plentiful."

As they walked, Kilik paid close attention to the path's details for future reference. In another couple of hours they reached their destination. Entering a small clearing, they found an old fire pit and a small cluster of makeshift shelters. The shelters were made of upright posts with sturdy branches lashed near their tops as crossbeam supports.

The shelters' roofs were made of leafy branches laid over the tops of the crossbeams.

"This is one of our oldest hunting and gathering camps," Kilik's father said. "We'll rest here, spend the night and get on with the hunt at first light tomorrow."

This was good news. Kilik felt more tired than he ever had in his short life. He lay down on a mat inside one of the shelters.

"But first we have to hunt for our supper," Solomol said just as the boy got comfortable. "A couple of squirrels or rabbits will do."

Kilik groaned.

"Unless you want to skip supper," his father added. "We could always do that."

Kilik dragged himself up and grabbed his hunting gear.

"Let's go," he said with little enthusiasm.

Off they went into the woods. Luckily for Kilik, they quickly came across a jackrabbit.

Kilik's first arrow hit the ground just behind the fast-moving hare. Digging deep to find one more burst of energy, the boy ran to catch the escaping creature. As he ran, Kilik pulled another arrow out of his quiver and let it fly. This time the projectile hit its moving mark.

"Yes!" he loudly exclaimed and retrieved his prize.

Meanwhile, his father had chased and killed a ground squirrel, so the two would have meat for dinner in addition to the dried berries and seeds they'd brought. This would help sustain and strengthen them for tomorrow's hunt for much larger game.

As the two finished their meal, Grandfather Sun headed home and Moon Woman rose into the darkening sky. Kilik had a hard time keeping his eyes open as fatigue overtook him. Soon his head began to nod, and the boy gave in to sleep. Meanwhile his father cleaned up the camp and put their gear away.

Before going to sleep himself, Solomol studied the moon and stars in the night sky. He did this every night, looking for signs that could tell him what tomorrow might bring. His eyes followed the bright band of stars across the middle of the sky, known among the Chumash as the place where human souls gather for a time in the afterlife.

Solomol's eyes moved further along this bright path, and that's when he saw them. Two thin, white rings completely circled the moon. Looking like double halos, they stood out in contrast to the dark sky and the distant stars.

"You don't see that very often," the experienced hunter said out loud.

Shaking Kilik's shoulders, Solomol woke up his son to show him this rare sign in the sky. Blinking the sleep from his eyes, the boy finally woke up enough to understand what his father was saying.

"Get up," Solomol said. "There's

something I need to show you."

Seeing the rings around the moon, Kilik said, "Moon is in her house tonight. Everybody knows it means we might have wind or rain tomorrow."

"That's what one ring would mean," his father corrected. "Two rings are more serious, I think, and very rare. If I remember correctly, many years ago the old village ceremonial leader said it meant a change was coming. Something bigger than wind or rain might be headed our way. Maybe not tomorrow, but soon."

Kilik was very tired and barely able to stay awake as his father spoke.

"Well, at least, whatever it is won't be happening tonight," the sleepy head said. He went back to his sleeping mat and quickly nodded off.

Solomol, on the other hand, was troubled late into the night.

He finally fell asleep wondering what big change might be coming their way. Would it be something good or something bad for the Chumash people?

Chapter 3 - The Strangers

At dawn, Solomol and Kilik climbed a small hill near the hunting camp. Kilik's father faced northward towards a medium-sized, grass covered hill visible in the distance.

"That's Shrine Mountain," he said. "Our people have journeyed to that place of prayer for generations. The top is covered with feathered prayer poles many years old. One day soon we'll go there together to do the same."

Just then Grandfather Sun peaked over an eastern ridge and the hunters greeted him with prayers for the day's hunt. Their goal was to bring down a deer or antelope that would feed many people at the festival. Prayers for a successful hunt could never hurt.

Chumash hunters often camouflaged themselves by wearing a deerskin or even the dried deer head with fake antlers. This allowed them to move closer to their prey without being noticed. Tightening the strap under his chin, Solomol made sure the deer head and fake antlers he had brought fit securely on his head.

Kilik's hunting disguise consisted of only a deerskin worn over his back and shoulders. It would require much more practice before the boy would be able to balance the dried skin and head of a dead deer on his head while attempting to stalk and kill a live one.

Quietly the pair of hunters approached a watering hole commonly used by thirsty animals in the area. Seeing that a young doe had stopped for a drink, Solomol signaled for his son to take the lead. This would be a good chance for Kilik to score his first kill.

32

With his arrow tightly drawn, the boy crept forward while hiding behind the cover of a row of bushes. Unfortunately, a dry branch snapped under his foot, sending a loud "crack" through the forest. The startled deer didn't wait to find out what had made the noise. She took off at high speed and quickly disappeared.

All Kilik could do is watch her go. He released a loud sigh of frustration.

"Don't worry," his father said. "You'll get the next one. Let's move back and wait for another animal to show up. It shouldn't take long."

And, of course, he was right. In no longer time than it takes a snake to swallow a field mouse, a young buck cautiously approached the watering hole.

Solomol signaled his son a second time. Stepping more carefully, Kilik once again used the bushes as cover. He waited until the animal dipped his head to drink, and then the boy made his move. Quickly standing upright, Kilik aimed and released his arrow like he'd done a thousand times in practice. And, like a thousand times before, the arrow found its mark.

Piercing the beast's side just behind the front leg, it sank deep into the chest. The shot was so well placed the animal never really knew what hit him. He fell and breathed his last few breaths on the spot.

Kilik ran to the fallen animal with his father close behind. They arrived in time to see the deer take his last breath. Immediately, Solomol placed his hand on the animal's head and said a quiet prayer, thanking the deer's spirit for sacrificing his life so the Chumash people would have food to eat.

"It's a proud moment, son," Solomol said. "You've crossed one of the important thresholds from childhood to manhood."

He reached out to the boy and drew him close in a fatherly embrace. Then he removed the talisman necklace from around his own neck and placed on Kilik's.

"This now belongs to you," his father said. "I received this from my father on my first hunt, and now I proudly hand it down to you."

Kilik was beyond excited. Not only had he made his first kill, but his father had passed on his most prized possession! No longer was Salapay the ideal Chumash man in Kilik's eyes. His own father was.

"Thank you, Father," Kilik said as he tried to hold in the emotion he felt. "I am glad I've made you proud. I hope I continue to do so."

"As you grow into manhood, you may be called upon to do more than hunt for food," Solomol added. "Your skills may also be needed to protect others in the tribe from an enemy. This requires real courage. So you must be prepared for that, as well."

Kilik realized this was a much more serious responsibility than just bringing home food.

"How do I build courage, Father?" he asked. "How will I know if I have it?"

"Courage comes from within you by joining your mind to your heart," Solomol replied. "If you love and respect those who need your protection, the courage you require will rise up in spite of any fear you feel."

Kilik looked away from his father, now feeling much smaller and less sure of himself than he did only a moment ago. His father sensed what his son was thinking.

"Don't worry about that now," he said in an encouraging voice. "There's plenty of time for you to practice the power to overcome fear. Plenty of time."

Kilik smiled at his father's words.

"You're starting to sound like Kimi," he said with a chuckle. "Repeating yourself. Repeating yourself."

They laughed at Kilik's little joke and turned their attention back to the task at hand. The man and the "almost-man" were ready to return home with their prize. First they needed to find and prepare a carrying pole to use for transporting the deer all the way back to the village.

"If we get this done quickly, we can be back home before dark," Solomol said. And so it was. Years of experience guided the Chumash hunter's every action, and soon the team was ready to return home.

Upon their arrival at the village, Solomol and Kilik presented the freshly killed deer to the village chief. Salapay and Tuhuy also took part in the presentation because they had contributed so much to Kilik's training.

Recognizing the boy's accomplishment, the chief congratulated Kilik on a job well done. The elder man also praised Kilik's father for raising such a good son, and then added another compliment on Solomol's arrow and bow-making abilities.

And as his final gesture of gratitude, the chief gave back a portion of the deer meat to Kilik's family for their evening meal.

"Our guests will start arriving for Hutash tomorrow," the chief said. "I'm happy to say that all our preparations are complete. So may we all have a blessed festival!"

With that, everyone returned to their homes. After preparing and seasoning the venison, Wonono roasted it over the open fire. The wonderful smell could be appreciated by all of their envious neighbors.

Salapay, Tuhuy and Tuhuy's mother, Yol, were all invited to eat with Kilik's family. They usually had such a good time when they were all together, but tonight it was different. All the adults could talk about was the double ring around the moon. The village astronomers, who always paid attention to everything that took place in the sky, had also seen this and were discussing its meaning.

Solomol's retelling of his friend's news about the strangers only added to their worry and concern. Could these two events coming so close together be related?

The following day, news of the strangers and the double moon rings were the talk of the village. Even as visitors began arriving for the festival, these discussions continued. And Chumash guests from other villages added fuel to the discussion because some had heard of the strangers as well and seen the double moon rings.

But as the ceremony began, the Chumash people put the news out of their minds. It was time for giving thanks and celebration. Following their ancient traditional ways, the people thanked Mother Earth for her bounty, celebrated a successful harvest and prayed for a bountiful harvest in the coming year.

On the third day of Hutash, however, unexpected guests arrived at the edge of the Place of River Turtles. Word of this arrival spread quickly through the gathering of festival participants. The odd strangers they'd just heard of and talked about were now present in their village!

When news of the strangers' arrival reached the ceremonial leaders, the Council of Twelve, the men called a temporary halt to the festivities. These leaders, also known simply as the Twelve, regularly worked with the unseen powers of the universe to keep harmony and balance within the Chumash worlds.

Stories of the strange newcomers included tales of unknown powers, so the Council of Twelve wanted an opportunity to judge these rumors for themselves. If the rumors were true, there could be much to learn about the mysterious ways of the strangers.

Although these were matters for adults to handle, Kilik and Tuhuy were determined to find out what was happening. So the pair edged their way through the crowd that had gathered around the uninvited guests.

The cousins found that these indeed were strange men. Their skin was rather pale. Three of the visitors wore long grey robes that covered their bodies entirely from the neck to their feet. One of the robed men, who had no hair on the top of his head, seemed to be in charge of the whole group.

About a dozen other men rode on the backs of tall, unknown four-legged beasts.

The outfits these men wore included hard material that covered the front and back parts of their bodies.

"Those hard shells make them look like turtles," Tuhuy whispered to Kilik. "I think we should call them turtle-men." The boys had a good, quiet laugh about that.

But the turtle-men also carried long cutting blades made of some hard, shiny material the boys had never seen. And along with the blades, the men also held long, straight sticks by their side. Kilik wondered if these were weapons of some kind. He would soon find out.

"What should we call the men in long robes?" Kilik asked.

"I don't know," Tuhuy replied. "We'll have to wait and see how they behave. The name we give them will tell of their qualities, like the name each of us receives from the elders."

What neither the two boys nor any of the Chumash onlookers knew was that these men were Spanish priests and soldiers who'd come to this land to build outposts for the Spanish empire. And these Spaniards brought with them the strong belief that the Chumash and other indigenous peoples were inferior human beings, in need of educating and civilizing in the ways of Europe.

Traveling with the strangers was a Native man from another region within the Chumash territory. Although he spoke a different Chumash tongue, his version of the language was close enough for the local Chumash to mostly understand what he said. He was the interpreter for the strangers. One of the robed men would say something, and this Native man would reveal what had been said.

"Priests and warriors these men are," the Native man proclaimed loudly. "From across ocean far they come to our lands. Good news bring to help our people. Make life better."

Upon hearing those words, the gathered Chumash talked among themselves, trying to determine what the speaker meant. Then one of the robed men said something, and a turtle-man got down off the back of his animal and stepped forward.

"Show you now power held by these men," the translator said.

The turtle-man raised his long stick and pointed it at a pile of gourds resting on the ground under a nearby oak tree. Suddenly, fire shot out of the end of the stick. At the same time, a crack of thunder rang out from it. Almost immediately, there was a loud "thwack" that came from the pile of gourds.

The whole crowd gasped and jumped back all at once at the fearful sight and sound. The people immediately burst into a loud chatter among themselves, expressing dismay and awe at what they'd just witnessed.

The turtle-man walked to the pile of gourds and picked one up. Holding the gourd up over his head, he pointed to the hole the stick-that-shoots-fire had made. The Native interpreter spoke.

"Fire-sticks these men use with power to kill," he said. "Better than bows, arrows and spears."

Kilik and Tuhuy had jumped back as far as anyone had when the fire-stick's thunder cracked through the air. The boys weren't sure if they should be in fear or in awe of what just happened.

"Are these powers from the Upper World or the Lower World?" the spokesman for the Twelve asked, expressing what many were thinking. "They certainly are not from this Middle World."

"From Man-in-sky come these things," the translator said. "These priest men invite your people to ceremony at their new camp west from here. Come share food, see more powers. Learn truth of their knowledge."

The Twelve gathered in a circle away from the strangers to talk about what they'd just seen and heard. They debated the events of the last few days. One reminded the group that the double moon rings foretold of great changes, not necessarily bad changes. Others spoke of the unusual powers displayed by the visitors. Surely men of such power and knowledge should be listened to and learned from, they said.

Finally, the spokesman for the Twelve reported to the gathered Chumash what the leaders had decided.

"If the things these men have said and shown us here today are true, then we may benefit from the knowledge they have," he said.

"A few of us are curious about these men and their powers. Therefore, we agree that some of us, not all, should respond to their invitation."

After hearing from their leaders, the people of the village and their invited Chumash guests began their own debate of these things.

Addressing the Native translator, the spokesman said, "Some of us will surely accept your invitation to see what these strange men bring among us. We shall arrive in three days, after the ceremony ends."

Kilik and Tuhuy just looked at one another for a moment. Tuhuy, the timid one, wasn't sure it was a good idea to go to the strangers' camp.

"What do you think we should do?" Tuhuy finally asked his cousin. "Should we stay in the village or travel to the strangers' camp to hear their talk and see more of their magic?"

"That will be decided by our parents or the chief," Kilik replied. "But as for me, I want to go. This may be the only chance in my lifetime to witness such curious events or strange powers. Something I have seen firsthand to tell my grandchildren about."

Chapter 4 - Buzzard Food

Kilik could hardly wait for Hutash to end. The ceremony leaders had promised to tell the villagers who would be traveling to the strangers' camp at the end of the festival.

In two more days, the festival ended and all the Chumash guests headed for their home villages. That night, by torchlight, the people of the Place of River Turtles gathered at the chief's home. The chief divided the people into two parts, those who would stay and those who would go.

The chief chose the families of Solomol and Salapay to travel to the strangers' camp along with the spokesman for the Twelve and a few of the elders. The chief said he wanted Kilik's father and uncle to go, because they were the village's two best protectors.

"All of you take your bows and spears and be ready to defend our people if the need arises," the chief said to the men who had been chosen.

When Kilik heard that his father and uncle would be going as protectors, the boy wanted to be included as a defender as well. He proposed this to his father.

"You said I would be called on one day to use my skills not just for hunting, but to protect our people, too," Kilik declared. "So I should take my bow and quiver of arrows on this trip, as well."

"Not yet," his father replied. "There are

other skills you must learn and practice before you're ready to take on that role."

"But, you said-"

"I meant someday soon," Solomol said firmly. "Not today!"

Kilik was not happy about this decision at all but realized that he'd have to prove himself to his father on this just as he'd done with hunting. So, he decided he'd wait and watch for an opportunity to do just that.

"Like it or not, I guess we're going to the strangers' camp," Tuhuy said to Kilik upon hearing the news.

"Look at it as an adventure," Kilik said to encourage his timid cousin. "A chance for you to travel further away from the village and see more of the valley you haven't seen before."

A group of about fifty people would be making the trip including several children.

Based on what the Native translator had said, it would be less than a full day's journey there. And so the following morning the group set out for the strangers' camp.

With their bows on one shoulder and quivers of arrows slung over the other, Solomol and Salapay took the lead. Several other men carried spears, as well. Their path took them westward along the river for a ways toward the ocean. Having never been far from their village, Kilik's sister, Stuk, was full of comments and questions.

"I don't think I like those turtle-men," she told her brother. "Don't like them. They didn't smile when they came to the village. Do you think they ever smile? I think they never smile. Never smile. And what are those big animals they were riding? They look like giant deer with no antlers. I've never seen anything like it." She prattled on and on like that until Kilik couldn't take it any more.

"Kimi, quiet down!" he yelled at her. "No one knows any more about the strangers or their animals or their smiles than you do. So just stop talking about it!"

He realized he'd been too harsh in his reaction and calmed himself down.

"I'm sorry, Stuk," he said quietly. "I didn't mean to yell at you. We're all a little nervous about this trip, so please just calm down. Okay? We'll get answers to our questions soon enough."

Solomol looked at his son approvingly, glad to see the boy was able to improve his attitude without needing guidance from a parent.

In the afternoon, the group turned northward away from the river and climbed a path that stretched up to the top of a flat hill. There they found the strangers' camp.

Gathering at the edge of the hill, the Chumash group waited politely until someone within the camp noticed them and invited them in. One of the turtle-men spied the group and notified the robed men that the people had arrived.

Two robed men and a group of turtle-men made a great show of welcoming their Chumash guests. One of the robed men, the one who had no hair on his head, spoke directly to the people from the Place of River Turtles. However, his attempts at speaking Chumash were crude and often incorrect.

"Haku," he said, using the familiar Chumash greeting. "Make you the priests and warriors here happy at arrival. Enter camp. Rest."

The robed priests escorted Kilik's people to the center of the camp and indicated that they should all sit down in an area where the grass had been cut short. As Kilik and Tuhuy followed their fathers, the boys studied their surroundings.

Many large oak trees on the property had been chopped down and cut into thinner, shorter lengths. Several of these pieces of the trees had been tied together to form a series of large frames. These frames had been covered with leafy branches to form shade shelters. A few of these shelters were scattered about the area.

Beyond the cluster of shelters were several large, stocky animals that were different than the animals ridden by the turtle-men. These unknown animals had horns on either side of their heads. But they weren't antlers like deer had. They were simpler, shorter horns that came to a single point. Kilik would learn later they were called cattle.

Looking beyond the area where the Chumash sat, Tuhuy saw other shelters a short distance away. But these were unlike the village homes the boy was familiar with.

These had straight walls with square door openings built with some sort of building blocks of uniform size. The walls were taller than any man, and seemed to be unfinished. It looked like they weren't finished being built yet.

It was while he was studying these walls that Tuhuy first noticed the other Indian people in the camp. He nudged Kilik and motioned for his cousin to see what he'd just seen. In the distance, a group of Native men, women and children were lined up waiting for something. Near the line stood a couple of the turtle-men holding their fire-sticks.

Looking closer, Kilik realized that the people were lined up to get some food from a woman who dished it out from a large container. He started to say something to Tuhuy, but was stopped when one of the robed men spoke in a loud voice.

"Eat now. Share bounty. Happy you came we are."

—

The priest then looked to the sky and began speaking his own odd language.

"He seems to be talking to the Sky People," Tuhuy said in a whisper. "I wonder if they can hear him. They don't speak his language."

Several Indian women carrying bowls of food then approached. At least it seemed like it might be food. It looked like nothing Kilik was used to eating. There bowls of some kind of soup, and brown squares that had been sliced into smaller pieces. Then a white liquid was brought out in large containers with handles.

There was none of the food Kilik was used to: no acorn soup, wild lettuce, roasted pine nuts or smoked deer meat. Finally, he saw something he recognized: plates of cooked fish with pink flesh. Salmon! Salmon were plentiful in the river that ran past Kilik's village at certain times of year. Some of his favorite stories were about the salmon.

He and Tuhuy tasted a little of everything and liked none of it but the salmon. After taking a few bites, Kilik's sister said, "This tastes like buzzard food, not people food. Buzzard food."

Kilik agreed.

As they picked at their food, Kilik continued to look over at the other Indians across the camp. He noticed that they were skinny, like they hadn't had enough to eat for a long time. They also looked tired and sad. Terribly sad.

Kilik wondered who those Natives were, where they had come from and why they were here. Just then, the bald-headed robed man spoke in his language to the Native translator who, in turn, made an announcement in his broken Chumash.

"Show you now new skills we have," he said. "These things to learn take time. Not right away."

The Chumash people were given a tour where they saw Indians from other tribes plowing a field at the far edge of the camp. One of the large horned animals pulled a device that cut through the soil. Others were making building blocks from mud and straw. Still others were stacking building blocks to create the wall of a square building. None of these activities was familiar to the Chumash villagers, and all of it looked like hard work.

Stuk was, of course, motivated to comment on every activity she witnessed. Her mother, however, strongly suggested that she keep her comments to herself for once.

As the tour continued, the translator said, "People you see come from another valley. Joined us, received knowledge, work here now."

Soon the tour came to an end, and Kilik saw that Grandfather Sun was heading for his home in the west.

The Chumash visitors talked among themselves about all the unfamiliar sights they'd seen that day. Some were curious about these activities and wanted to learn more about them. Others didn't see the value of what they'd been shown and were ready to return to their village homes.

"I believe our people have seen enough for one day," the tribal spokesman said to the Indian translator who stood near by. "We should be heading back to our village. It will be dark soon so we need to find a good place to camp for the night."

The translator repeated the message to the bald priest in the strangers' tongue.

"Stay night here," the priest said without need of the translator. "Lessons begin in morning, starting with words of Man-in-Sky."

"We prefer to come back for lessons another time," the Chumash spokesman replied.

Seeing that Kilik's people weren't convinced they should stay, the bald-headed robed man then withdrew something from a bag that hung from his shoulder. With the flair of a magician he held up for everyone to see several strands of beads. The little pieces of brightly colored glass caught the light from the setting sun. These glimmering pieces of cut glass were more colorful and beautiful than the shell beads made and used as money by the Chumash for centuries. Everyone from the Place of Turtles moved in to more closely examine these sparkling beauties.

All the while this conversation had been going on, the turtle-men quietly surrounded the Chumash visitors trying to not draw attention to themselves. They moved into place to make sure that the people of Kilik's village were unable to leave no matter what.

"You be paid well for work you join us," the translator said, indicating the colorful strings of beads. The priests had already learned that the Chumash made and used beads for money so they brought many strands of them from Spain.

The Chumash people began discussing the matter among themselves but could not achieve agreement. Seeing that more convincing was needed, the priest talked some more to the translator.

"Only want best for you," the translator said. "Good you stay here, learn new ways. Accept words of Man-in-sky. "

Not knowing what the priest and soldiers really had in mind, the villagers finally agreed that it couldn't hurt to stay for a few days to learn more about the strangers and their ways. They had no reason to believe that the priests had no intention of ever letting Kilik's people leave this camp.

Chapter 5 - What's Going on Here?

The turtle-men began separating the Chumash into smaller groups without explaining why. Kilik saw that young children were placed with their parents into one group. Stuk, who wanted to stay close to Kilik, was made to stand next to Solomol and Wonono. Older girls and young unmarried women were put into another group. Kilik and Tuhuy were placed with a couple of older boys and a young single man from the village.

"What's going on?" Kilik asked his father. "Why are they separating us?"

Before Solomol could say anything, the translator answered. "It's for sleeping while here at camp," the man said. "Easier to protect everyone and make sure all are where they belong."

"We can sleep anywhere under the blanket of stars," Solomol said. "Mother Moon watches over us."

"Not here," the translator said. "You learn more how priests do things beginning tomorrow morning."

Then the turtle-men moved the separate groups to different parts of the camp. Kilik, Tuhuy and the other older boys were taken to a shelter where other young Indian men were gathered. This shelter was one of the partially completed buildings Tuhuy had noticed earlier. These young men all wore a one-piece garment made of some kind of loosely woven material.

Kilik strained to see where the rest of his family had been taken. He caught a glimpse of them as they were placed in an area where other families were gathered. Uncle Salapay and Aunt Yol were with them, too. Their shelter was merely a shaded covering made of tree trunks and leafy branches.

Then Kilik and Tuhuy were each given their own one-piece garment. A turtle-man motioned to the other young men who already wore these garments, indicating that Kilkik and Tuhuy were to put these on. Noticing that the cloth was rough and scratchy, the boys decided not to. Kilik tossed his garment on the ground. He wasn't about to put that uncomfortable covering on!

The turtle-man gruffly barked some angry words at Kilik and pushed him down to the dirt next to the garment. Kilik got the message. He picked up the garment, stood up and put it on. Tuhuy did so as well.

At that moment, a loud clanging noise rang out from somewhere across the camp.

It was almost as loud as the thunder that came from the fire-stick the turtle-man used back in their village.

"What was that noise?" Tuhuy asked one of the other young men in their group. The boy responded by speaking a Native language Tuhuy did not understand. He must be from another tribe, Tuhuy thought.

As the sky darkened, the turtle-man lit a torch that allowed him to see what he was doing. Kilik noticed other torches being lit across the camp.

The turtle-man handed Kilik and Tuhuy blankets to lie on. They saw the other young men were already in the process of spreading their own blankets on the ground and getting ready to go to sleep. The Chumash boys reluctantly followed their example. Seeing that the new boys were adequately following directions, the turtle-man left, taking his torch with him.

—

Kilik and Tuhuy lay there in the dark next to one another. "This covering is too scratchy to wear all night," Tuhuy whispered. "I'm going to take mine off."

"Good idea," Kilik agreed. The boys each removed the garment, which was like a long shirt.

"That's better," Kilik said. "I think I might be able to sleep now."

"I don't think I can," Tuhuy said. "Things get stranger and stranger the longer we are here. I think we should all go home tomorrow." But the experiences of the day had been exhausting and the cousins soon fell asleep.

At dawn the next morning the loud clanging noise rang across the camp. Over in the shelter where the parents and children stayed, the men awoke to find their weapons gone. They had laid their bows and spears beside them for sleeping.

"You have stolen our weapons!" Salapay accused a nearby turtle-man. "Return them at once."

Two turtle-men moved in on Kilik's uncle, blocking him from moving in any direction.

"Calm down," the translator said as he approached. "You won't need them while you are here. We are peaceful men here, but our warriors keep everyone in order."

"I demand that we be released now and allowed to return to our homes," Solomol said as he moved to stand next to his brother.

Hearing the commotion, the head priest came and spoke to the translator.

"Man-in-sky has delivered you to us," the translator said. "And here you and your people will stay."

The two turtle-men standing guard over Salapay and Solomol pointed their fire-sticks at the men's heads. The Chumash men then understood what would happen if they continued their protest.

Across the camp, Kilik awoke from sleep. Turtle-men entered the young mens' area and made sure all were waking up. Somehow Tuhuy had slept through all the noise. One of the turtle-men shook him harshly and barked commands at him. Kilik rushed to the man and tried to push him away.

"You keep your hands off him," Kilik shouted at the man, grabbing his arm. "There's no need to be so rough."

Almost growling at Kilik, the strong man swung the boy through the air several feet. Kilik landed on the dirt floor with a loud groan. That particular noise finally woke Tuhuy.

"Hey, what's going on?" he said loudly, seeing his cousin lying on the floor in pain. The turtle-man picked Tuhuy up off his mat and stood him up.

Then he picked up the garment where Tuhuy had left it and thrust it at the boy, motioning for him to put it on. He did the same to Kilik, standing nearby to make sure they did as they had been told.

After the boys had their garments on, the turtle-man pointed his fire-stick toward the doorway, indicating that the boys should get moving.

The pair fell in line with the others as they walked single-file out of the room. Trudging toward the clearing in the camp where the Chumash had first gathered, the young men joined the rest of the Indians who had gathered.

The bald-headed priest and his translator waited there. Behind them stood a large wooden symbol made of two crossed logs that had been tied together. The translator spoke to the Chumash people.

"Today you be blessed to begin new life," he said. "Leave savage ways behind and receive new name."

The bald-headed priest signaled to the turtle-men who gathered around Kilik's people. The priest sat down at a table containing a stack of white leaves that he made marks on. Beginning with the tribal spokesman, the turtle-men put the Chumash people into a single-file line. Each person in the line was taken before the priest.

Kilik and Tuhuy couldn't hear or understand what was being said but saw that the bald-headed priest spoke a few words to each member of Kilik's village in his odd language. Then the translator said a few words in Chumash. Finally, the villager would attempt to imitate what the priest had said in the unknown language.

The priest then sprinkled some water on the villager's head, made markings on the white leaves, and made a final statement to the villager. A turtle-man led the villager away as another Chumash person was brought before the priest.

Tuhuy stood in front of his cousin in the line, and finally his turn came to go before the priest. However, Kilik quickly stepped in front of Tuhuy.

"Let me go next," the boy said protectively. "Watch and listen to what happens so you'll know what to expect."

Kilik walked up to the priest's table to undergo his turn in the process. Standing before the priest, the translator told Kilik to repeat what the priest said. The priest spoke some gibberish that made no sense. Kilik didn't understand what was expected of him. A turtle-man standing nearby poked the boy in the ribs with a fire-stick.

"Ouch!" Kilik exclaimed. "What did you do that for?"

"Repeat priest's words so you become a member of camp," the translator said.

"I'm not interested in becoming a member of your camp," Kilik replied. "I have a home, and I'm ready to go back there."

The translator interpreted the boy's words for both the priest and the turtle-man. The turtle-man moved close to Kilik and pointed his fire-stick towards the sky. Thunder roared in Kilik's ears as the soldier fired the weapon very close to him.

"Ahhh!" the boy screamed as he covered his ears and buckled over in agony. All activity in the camp ceased as everyone turned his attention in Kilik's direction. Kilik's concerned parents tried to move towards their son, but were stopped by the soldier closest to them.

The translator spoke again to Kilik.

"Last night people agreed to stay here. Now is time you agree to follow teaching and obey priest. Once again I say repeat priest's words."

Kilik stood up, his ears still ringing.

He tried to listen closely to the sounds coming out of the priest's mouth. He tried as best he could to imitate those sounds even though they were all meaningless. The priest smiled as he sprinkled a few drops of water on Kilik's head.

"Now you are reborn as one of us, and you will no longer take part in your old ways," the translator said. "You begin new life and learn to speak and live in ways that are pleasing to Man-in-sky."

The priest spoke again as he made marks on the white leaves. "Now you be called Miguel," the translator interpreted. "Say it: Miguel."

Seeing that the turtle-man stood ready to jab him again in the ribs, Kilik obediently repeated the strange word, "Mee-gel."

"Good," the priest said, and immediately the turtle-man escorted the boy away. Kilik turned back in time to see Tuhuy step toward the priest. Fear was on his cousin's face.

"Just do what they say, and you'll be all right," Kilik said. "Nothing to be afraid of." The turtle-man gruffly pushed Kilik ahead of him, causing the boy to trip over a tree root. He fell to the ground.

Lying there on the ground examining the scrape on his knee, Kilik realized something. Overnight he and his people had gone from being guests to being prisoners.

Chapter 6 - Coyote-Men

Kilik's father had been ushered over to the area where all the Indians in the camp had been gathered. There the bald-headed priest was making some sort of speech in his foreign tongue in front of the crossed logs. In a kind of early morning ritual, the Indians were all kneeling on the ground either bowing their heads or looking at the priest.

Seeing his son trip and fall, Solomol stood from his kneeling position and ran the short distance to help Kilik up. He saw the look of confusion on his son's face, the same confusion all the people from the Place of River Turtles were experiencing.

"Are you all right?" he asked his son, checking the red spot on Kilik's side were the turtle-man had poked him and the scrape on his knee.

"Father, what is this place?" the boy asked. "Why are they treating us as prisoners? I thought we were guests."

Before Solomol could answer, the turtle-man who pushed Kilik shouted something at them and motioned for them to separate. Pointing in the direction Solomol had come from, the soldier indicated that he was to return there. The Chumash man ignored him.

"Our tribal spokesman knows one of the men from the other tribe and can speak some of their language," Solomol said to his son. "These men mean to keep us here and make us work for them."

Just then the soldier hit Solomol on the side of the head with the fat end of his fire-stick.

Kilik's father fell to the ground in the same place Kilik had fallen.

"Father!" Kilik yelled as he stooped beside him. The turtle-man jerked the boy up by the arm and barked more words at him. Pushing the twelve-year old towards the gathering place, the soldier didn't allow Kilik time to see if his father, who wasn't moving, was all right. Kilik was briskly marched off to the gathering of Indians where he was closely watched by the soldier.

Soon afterwards, Tuhuy was brought to the kneeling area as well.

"Now I know what to call the robed men," he said as he sat on the ground next to Kilik. "They are tricksters and liars, telling us that they've come to help us and teach us when what they really want to do is imprison us and work us. I think they are coyotes disguised as men. They are coyote-men."

Kilik laughed at his cousin's comment,

and it felt good to laugh. Tuhuy, on the other hand, didn't see the humor in their situation.

"Cousin, you're as clever as ever," Kilik said. "Faced with a fearful situation, you're still able to use your mind to look at things a different way."

That's when the nearby turtle-man slapped Kilik in the back of the head and said, "Shhhh."

And thus the "new life" they had been promised began - as slaves of the Spanish mission system in a place the Spaniards called Alta California.

Like the two hundred or so other Indians around them, Kilik and Tuhuy knelt in the grass in the early dawn light as the bald-headed coyote-man droned on up in front. From time to time the man looked at the white leaves he held that had been tied together within a black covering.

In a while the loud clanging noise rang

---

out again, and the Indians that already lived in the camp stood up in response to the noise. They moved in line toward a large table set up under one of the brush shelters.

The Chumash newcomers followed the line and received a bowl filled with a mush that definitely wasn't acorn soup, along with a slice of bread. Kilik and Tuhuy had never seen bread either. But, following the lead of the other Indians, they sat down and ate the strange tasting food.

The loud clanging came again soon and the Indians in camp began moving again. The young Indian man who'd been nearest Kilik and Tuhuy when they went to bed came over and motioned for the boys to follow him. The translator was waiting for them near the half-finished building where they'd slept.

"This young man is José," he said to the Chumash boys. "He show you how to do your job, to make pieces used to build houses needed here at this camp."

Then the translator spoke to José in the strangers' language, which the young Indian man understood. As the translator spoke, he mentioned Kilik's new name "Miguel" and pointed to Kilik. Then he pointed to Tuhuy and said, "Rafael."

"That's supposed to be my new name," Tuhuy whispered in Kilik's ear.

But Kilik would have none of it.

"I am Kilik, and this is Tuhuy," he said to the translator and the young Native. "I have not changed my name, and neither has my cousin."

"Best if you never mention old names in front of the soldiers or priests," the translator said. "You be punished."

Kilik didn't know what to say to that, so he said nothing.

"Now go with José and learn job he does," the translator said. "Just keep busy and you won't get into trouble."

The Chumash boys realized it was best to follow orders for now, and talk about it all later that night.

José motioned for the boys to follow him, and he headed for the southern edge of the camp. There, in a flat open area, the boys found row-upon-row of frames lying on the ground. These wooden frames were about twice the length of a man's foot and half as wide. Some of the frames were empty, but others contained a hard tan brown substance that looked like a brick.

Kilik and Tuhuy watched as a few Indian men and boys began their day's work. Some were mixing water, dirt and dried grass together. Others were pouring the mixture into empty frames. Still others were removing frames from the brown rectangles that had dried in the sun. All this was being done under the watchful eye of one of the turtle-men.

José walked over to one of the dry frames

and shook it. Then he lifted frame, and it separated from its contents. Setting aside the frame, he picked up the brown block and said, "adobe." Taking a few nearby adobe blocks, the young man stacked a few one on top of the other.

Kilik and Tuhuy began to get the picture. They were going to be making the building blocks used to construct the buildings in the camp. It looked like hard work.

José motioned for the boys to once again follow him. He walked to the edge of the adobe-making grounds where several wooden containers had been stacked. Picking up one of the containers, he said, "bucket," using the language of the strangers. He indicated that Kilik and Tuhuy should each take one.

Jose nodded his head in a southerly direction and started walking. That's when the boys realized they'd be hauling buckets of water from the river to the adobe-making area.

"Don't even think about run away," a voice said, coming from behind them. It was the translator. "You be captured and brought back. Punished." He let that sink into the boys' minds before turning and heading back for the main camp.

Kilik and Tuhuy looked at one another in dismay. "We're trapped here," Tuhuy said with a shocked look on his face. "And there's nothing anyone can do about it."

Kilik tried to think of something to say that might make their situation not seem so hopeless, but nothing came to mind.

Just then José, who was ahead of them several yards, whistled to the boys and yelled something they didn't understand. What they did understand was that they were supposed to follow him to the river to fetch pails of water.

And they also understood that they're carefree days of hunting, fishing and playing together were definitely over.

Chapter 7 - The Bells

At dawn each day, the loud clanging noise awoke all the Indian laborers from their night of fitful sleep. Kilik and Tuhuy came to learn that the clanging noise came from something called bells. And these bells ruled their lives. The bells signaled the time to wake, the time to eat, the time to work, the time to study and the time for sleep. Clang, clang, ding, dong. All through the day. Each and every day.

As the days wore on, the Chumash people begin to understand more of the words spoken by the strangers' in their foreign language. At first the process was simple.

A soldier would bark out a word of command and then act out what he meant or physically push you into the action he wanted you to perform. Certain words were repeated several times a day. "Awake, kneel, pray, eat, work, obey, march, be quiet, listen, eyes forward, sleep."

Kilik and Tuhuy learned that the place they now lived and worked was called a mission. The three coyote-men who were in charge of everything were Padre Fiero, Padre Aspero and Padre Espíritu. The head turtle-man was named El Capitan Castigar.

The collections of white leaves with markings were called books. And the black book the padres often read from was called the Bible. The padres said this Bible contained all the words ever spoken by Man-in-sky, also known as God, to humans. And humans could only know God's power through the Bible.

This, too, made no sense to Kilik for tribal elders taught that spiritual power existed throughout the world. This power could be used to help people if you knew how to read the stars and how to listen to the spirit within every rock, plant, tree and animal.

But no one dared to question or contradict the coyote-men.

Over the weeks and months that followed, Kilik's people <u>had</u> to learn the ways and words of their captors. Things that had no place in Chumash daily life but were all important to the Spaniards' sense of civilization.

The women and girls learned how to wash clothes for the soldiers and padres in the outdoor laundry that had been built by Indian labor. They learned to use the loom the strangers had brought with them to weave the scratchy garments each of them had to wear. And there was the planting and harvesting of vegetables in gardens located near their sleeping quarters. Finally, they learned to cook for everyone in the mission, fine dishes for the priests and soldiers–tasteless paste for the Indians.

In addition to the adobe brickmaking that Kilik and Tuhuy were engaged in, the men learned new skills as well. They were the ones who built and painted and maintained all the buildings on the mission grounds. And daily they worked the nearby fields planting, plowing and harvesting grains.

There was the care, feeding and slaughtering of the cattle. The men also treated the cattle hides to transform them into leather, which they worked into saddles, reins and boots for the soldiers. Indian men also learned to be blacksmiths who made all things metal, like nails, hinges, and plows.

It was during meals that Kilik and Tuhuy got to visit with their families. These were short interactions where everyone spoke in hushed tones in hopes they wouldn't be punished for speaking their own language. These were times when mothers could comfort their daughters and sons or tend to their wounds of the day. These were times when fathers could speak words of encouragement to their children so they wouldn't lose hope. Children were also reminded to not forget who they were or where they came from. Chumash fathers and mothers were not sure they could even follow these words themselves.

It was at one such meal that Kilik's father had whispered that he and Salapay were worried that other people from their village might come looking for them. If they did, those people would also become captives, too. Salapay hoped to devise a plan to warn them to stay away.

Kilik, on the other hand, was worried about his little sister. Stuk and the other young

Chumash children had lessons every day so they could learn to talk the language of the strangers. And they were told stories that came from the black book.

What bothered Kilik about it all was the way this was affecting her. Gone was her free-spirited chattiness. Gone was her outgoing nature. What had replaced those things was her retreat from other people. She no longer kidded her older brother. She no longer mocked him with her playful taunts. That had been her way. That had been their relationship. All those things were now mere memories of the past.

All those things had been replaced by the rules.

The coyote-men, who expected to be called padre or father, had many rules for the Indians to follow, rules that made no sense to Kilik or any of the Natives.

These were rules that even the priests'

people back in their home country did not have to follow.

Young single men and women had to be separated so they couldn't and wouldn't become attracted to one another. Prayers while kneeling had to be said every morning and every evening. The black book had to be studied every night before sleep time. The scratchy clothing that created sores on the Indians' skin had to be worn at all times. Every order of every priest and soldier had to be obeyed without question.

Kilik and Tuhuy saw what happened to those who disobeyed the rules. The padres believed that the Indians of all ages were mere children and had to be treated as such. The only way to make these children behave and obey the rules was by physical punishment, they believed. So, you could be severely whipped if you didn't do your work or if you tried to secretly meet with friends.

If you ran away, they could lock up your feet in something called the "stocks" or hobble your feet like they did to horses to keep them from escaping.

Indians who managed to escape and return to their villages were hunted down, captured and dragged back to the mission. And if the village refused to give up the escapee, soldiers burnt the place to the ground, leaving the people to rebuild as best they could.

One man from the Place of River Turtles did manage to escape the mission and make it back home. While there, he was able to report what had happened to the original group of Chumash who'd left to visit the strangers' camp.

But the following day, soldiers rode into the village looking for the man. He hid in the nearby woods as the turtle-men ransacked the village in their search. This time, instead of burning the village, the soldiers rounded up a dozen or so people and tied them together in a line. Those left behind watched in horror as their fellow tribesmen were marched away.

In the mission, speaking your Native language earned you a particularly distasteful punishment. It was as if those words in and of themselves were dirty and evil. Once, in a rare moment of joy when the cousins were remembering the fun they'd had playing hoop-and-pole, Tuhuy had shouted out a few words in the Chumash language. Unfortunately, Father Aspero overheard that expression of Native joy and grabbed the boy by the ear. Dragging him before Father Fiero, the padre reported Tuhuy's sin. Two soldiers were summoned to hold the boy down as the head priest washed his mouth out with soap. Salapy and Yol could only stand by and helplessly watch as this punishment was carried out.

It was at this moment that Tuhuy's father vowed to take action. Somehow. Some way. Some day.

Chapter 8 - The Secret Plan

Since the padres and the soldiers couldn't watch every Indian laborer all the time, they had devised a plan to select certain Indians to watch other Indians instead. The padres picked out Natives that had been in the mission awhile and had learned how to speak pretty good Spanish.

Within prison systems, these chosen ones are known as trustees. Not only do trustees make sure fellow prisoners are following the rules, but they also report back to the warden, the head of the prison, any wrong doing by the inmates. So it was inside the missions, as well.

While making a show of this being a special honor for the chosen trustees, the priests also made it known that any disobedience would result in severe punishment, not only for the offending trustee, but also for the trustee's family. That provided ample incentive for the chosen ones to follow orders even though that often meant causing pain or grief to a fellow Indian.

After Tuhuy's mouth had been washed out with soap, and his father came to the conclusion he must take action, some of the braver Chumash men began meeting in secret at night to figure out a way to escape from their miserable existence.

Late at night, when they were certain the soldiers were asleep in their quarters, Salapay and Solomol would quietly sneak out of their rooms and meet others at a pre-arranged location in the woods.

After a few nights of these meetings, a few other Chumash from other villages heard about the gatherings and joined in.

All-in-all about a dozen men met to create an escape strategy. All discussions had to be conducted in whispers so as not to disturb sleeping priests and soldiers. One-by-one ideas were proposed and then discarded when a flaw in that plan was discovered.

Having heard several ideas that had potential, Salapay came up with a way of combining the best parts of these to create a cohesive plan that might work. He knew from observation of the soldiers what their daily routines were. He also knew they kept their weapons, ammunition and supplies in a special storeroom that was located at the far end of the mission grounds.

The first part of Salapay's plan called for himself and a few men from the nearest villages to escape and travel to their homes.

There they would enlist the help of the men in those villages to come back and free the captives. They realized that not all of the men would be successful in bringing back warriors. But with the help of about fifty men from a few nearby villages, there would be enough manpower to overwhelm the mission soldiers. Then everyone could be freed.

Part two of the plan called for the other men among the planners who remained in the mission to attack the soldiers from behind. The soldiers would have to deal with attacks from both outside and inside the mission, and this would hopefully create enough confusion to allow the Indians to take control. Salapay would be the one from the Place of River Turtles to run back home, while Solomol would stay behind to lead the attack from within.

Salapay and Solomol decided that the plan should be carried out on night of the next full moon. This would give the escapees enough light to pick their way through the underbrush and get far from the mission as quickly as possible.

One evening during their skimpy dinner, the two Chumash fathers explained in hushed tones the plans to their sons.

"That sounds far too dangerous," Tuhuy said to his father. "You could get caught or killed trying to carry out that plan."

"It's a father's duty to take risks in order to protect his family and his people," Salapy replied. "I have failed to do either ever since we came to this place." He hugged his son close and then continued. "You must stay close to Kilik after I leave. You two boys are best when you work together."

When Kilik heard of the plan, he said, "Father, I know I can help you overcome the soldiers here in the mission when the attack comes. Don't leave me out of this."

Using a stern voice Kilik had seldom heard, Solomol replied, "What I expect of you is to become the protector and leader of your sister, your cousin and the other children if something should happen to me. They'll need someone they can count on here. You're that someone."

Kilik started to protest but realized that this was an important course of action for him. This was something he could set his mind to and carry out if needed.

"All right, Father," he said. "I will accept this as my duty, and I will not fail." He hugged his father tightly, and then the two separated before being noticed by one of the soldiers.

When the appointed night to carry out the plan came, Solomol quietly said goodbye to his wife and daughter, and Salapay bid farewell to his wife. Keeping low and quiet, the two crept over to the meeting place they'd set with the other men. It was a small cluster of trees beyond the eastern border of the mission.

They waited a short while until all but one of their co-conspirators, a fellow named Reynaldo, arrived.

"Has anyone seen Reynaldo tonight," Solomol asked the men in the group in a whisper. No one had.

"Well, we can't wait any longer," Salapay said. "We must head out now." With everyone in agreement, the men prepared to set out on their separate paths. All of a sudden, a gruff voice came out from the darkness.

"You men are going nowhere," El Capitan Castigar said. "We know all about your plans for escape." With that, about a dozen soldiers stepped from their hiding places in the brush, surrounding the Chumash men. Castigar carried a torch, which he now lit. Light from the flame revealed Reynaldo standing beside him.

"Reynaldo here, has been a very good spy," the captain said in a much friendlier voice. "He and his family will be rewarded for their loyalty to the padres." Then his voice returned to the gruff tone again. "The rest of you will receive ample punishment for your efforts," he roared. Soldiers seized the Native men and ushered them back to the mission's main plaza.

The following morning Kilik and Tuhuy awoke horrified to find their fathers locked in the stocks. These locking devices sat on the ground designed to hold a person in place at both ankles. The person being punished had to sit or lie on the ground in this uncomfortable position for as long as the priests deemed necessary.

Both boys ran to their fathers, but were prevented from reaching them.

"Keep away," the guarding soldier commanded. "No one is to come near them, so go on about your business."

Speaking in Chumash, Salapay said to the boys, "Remember what we told you. Stay together. Stay strong."

"Come, boys," Wonono called out. She and Tuhuy's mother, Yol, had been standing among the Indians at the edge of the plaza, kept in place by another soldier. The boys ran to their mothers.

Just then Father Fiero and Captain Castigar approached the men in stocks. The priest spoke in a whisper to the captain who grinned and said, "Right away, Father." Turning to one of his men, he barked out a command. "Bring me the flogging whips!" he ordered.

The turtle-man rushed to the soldiers' quarters and returned in a few minutes. In place of the rifle he usually held, he now carried two flogging whips. These whips were different than usual whips. Instead of having one length of braided leather, these consisted of several shorter strands of leather. A barb was tied to the end of each strand.

Two other soldiers unlocked Solomol and Salapay from the stocks and pushed them towards a large tree that stood in the mission plaza. Several soldiers worked to tie Kilik's and Tuhuy's fathers to the tree in a standing position with their faces towards the tree. Then Reynaldo stepped into the plaza and approached the soldier who had the whip.

"From among you we have chosen our favored ones who act as our eyes and ears when we're not present," Father Fiero announced. "Reynaldo here is one such trustee. He will have the honor of helping to mete out God's punishment today."

Yol and Wonono both realized what was about to happen. "No!" they screamed and ran toward the tree. A third soldier stepped in front of them, grabbing the women by their arms. He escorted the women back to her places next to their sons. The two sets of mothers and sons hugged each other tightly, turning away from the unfolding scene.

"These men were identified as the organizers of the attempted escape," Father Fiero, the head priest, said. "And so, they will bear the brunt of punishment on behalf of all those who took part."

He paused and looked at those Natives around him. He was sure this day would not be soon forgotten by this bunch of inferior human beings in this most remote outpost of the great Spanish empire!

"Get on with it," he ordered, and the flogging began. Reynaldo raised the whip and brought it down on Salapay's back with a sharp "thwack." A soldier did the same to Solomol. The men yelped in pain with each stroke as it tore into their flesh. The crowd of Natives, forced to watch, groaned in agony with each crack of the whips.

Thirty blows were meted out, leaving the two Chumash men ragged, bloody messes.

Their tortured bodies sagged against the ropes that held them to the tree. Soldiers cut the ropes, and both Solomol and Salapay fell to the ground unconscious.

"My children, I feel no joy in carrying out this punishment," Father Fiero said to the assembled crowd of Natives. "But when God's children betray his trust, we must act. It is for your own good. And so this lesson ends for now."

Wonono, Yol, Kilik and Tuhuy broke from the crowd, and this time the soldiers allowed them to rush to the fallen men. Other Native women rushed to help them with dry cloths to wipe away the blood.

Father Espíritu, a quiet man who seldom spoke, stepped from his position behind the head priest. He also started to move toward the beaten men.

"Those men need medical attention right away," the kindly Espíritu said.

Father Fiero put a hand out to stop him. "Let the Natives tend to them," Fiero ordered.

"But we have the medical supplies needed to properly treat their wounds," Espíritu protested.

Father Fiero turned to face the protesting priest.

"You are never to contradict my order," he said firmly. "Especially in front of the Indians. It undermines my authority."

"Your punishments are far too cruel!" Espíritu said. "And not appropriate for the training of new followers of the faith. I'll be writing a full complaint to head of missions in Mexico City." He stomped off in anger before the head priest could say another word.

Fiero followed Espíritu to the priests' quarters, leaving the Natives in a state of shock. Kilik and Tuhuy watched the head priest as he left the plaza, their eyes burning with hatred for the cruel man. Father Fiero was right about one thing. Kilik, Tuhuy and the others would not forget what he'd done that day.

The following day, one of the turtle-men approached Kilik and Tuhuy as they worked in the field. The man said that Father Espíritu wished to see them right away. The boys feared that they too were to be punished just for being the sons of the escape planners.

"I'm sure you boys are wondering why I asked to see," the priest said after dismissing the soldier.

"What have we done wrong, Father?" Tuhuy asked with worry in his voice.

"You've done nothing wrong, boys" Espíritu replied. "I merely want to ask you a question."

The cousins both released huge sighs of relief.

"Each of us padres have one or two youth who work as our assistants," the priest explained. "To run errands, help us with chores.

That sort of thing."

"Yes," Kilik said. "We've noticed that a few of us have been lucky enough to get those jobs. Seems easier than working in the fields."

"Would either or both of you be interested in becoming my assistant?" the padre asked.

"Who wouldn't?" the boys answered at the same time.

"Good," Espíritu said. "I've gotten special permission from Father Fiero to have two assistants instead of just one. And I've felt bad for you both ever since your fathers were whipped in the plaza. I believe the head priest here goes too far when correcting the behavior of the newer members of our flock."

"Every Indian in this place would probably agree with you, Father," Kilik said too boldly. Realizing he shouldn't be talking badly about the head priest to Indians, Espíritu changed the subject.

"You boys finish your regular duties in the field today, and then report to me after morning prayers tomorrow," Espíritu said. "I think we'll get along fine. Now run along. I'll see you tomorrow."

Kilik and Tuhuy couldn't believe their good luck. They ran back to the married couples' quarters where their mothers were still tending to their fathers' wounds to share the good news. But they quickly returned to their labors in the fields so as not to also receive punishments.

In the days that followed, Kilik and Tuhuy heard Espíritu and Fiero argue more than once about how the Indians were being treated and when they might be free to return to their former lives. Since the boys could now understand most of what was being said, they realized that not all of the strangers were in favor of acting so cruelly towards the Native people. They also learned that the original mission plan called for the Indians to be released after they'd been "civilized."

Not that this information meant anything would change, but Kilik and Tuhuy felt the first little rays of hope in their hearts. Maybe their lives and the lives of their families could one day return to normal. They could always hope.

Chapter 9 - A Small Vacation

Time passed as Solomol and Salapay recovered from their whippings. But ever since witnessing the severe public floggings, none of the Native laborers felt like working as hard as they had before. And the usual punishments really had no effect in correcting this behavior. The priests could see that their laborers were more depressed than ever and less productive than ever.

After repeated arguments and pleas, Father Espíritu was able to convince the head priest to allow the Natives a small vacation.

Father Fiero agreed to allow a few Indians at a time to visit their traditional food gathering sites and home villages–with, of course, an escort of mission soldiers led by Captain Castigar. So, under guard of a full contingent of turtle-men, Kilik and the people of his village could journey to one of their traditional fishing sites to catch fish. Then they could travel to one of their local camps to collect acorns as they'd always done.

To the people from the Place of the River Turtles it was a glorious day. They set out from the mission after their usual morning meal of tasteless paste and headed south. The adults carried wooden bowls or baskets loaned to them by the mission priests. And during the journey, the soldiers even allowed them to speak to one another in their Native tongue.

As they walked, Kilik and Tuhuy picked up small stones and threw them at fleeing ground squirrels, pretending to be on a hunting trip. Stuk, who stayed close to her mother, looked for ladybugs and other small insects on the leaves of familiar plants.

Their parents walked arm-in-arm along a part of a trail they'd used hundreds of times in better days. They dared to allow themselves to forget their prison labors within the mission.

When they reached the river, the children immediately jumped in. Kilik and Tuhuy splashed each other with handfuls of the cool refreshing water. Their regular baths of bygone days had almost become a forgotten memory.

Quickly weaving makeshift nets from nearby vines, the men waded into the river to snare salmon and other fish. The women spread out along the riverbanks to search for wild lettuce and other edible plants.

After about an hour of splashing and fishing, Kilik's group decided to move on toward one of their traditional acorn-gathering areas close by. They didn't know if they'd ever be allowed to prepare the acorns to make them suitable for acorn soup, but it just felt so good to be gathering, to be in the midst of the natural world.

They filled their bowls and baskets to the brim and then took everything to the middle of the old camp. This camp was similar to the one Kilik and Solomol had stayed in during Kilik's one and only hunting trip. Lighting a fire in the old fire pit, the women skewered the salmon on long sticks for cooking.

When the fish were done cooking, several of the soldiers rushed to the fire pit and helped themselves to the feast, pushing aside the women who'd done the cooking. The Chumash could do nothing but watch the men gorge themselves and then eat what was left.

"Now we will visit your home village," Captain Castigar announced. "You need to move along quickly so we can get back to the mission."

Kilik and Tuhuy couldn't believe their ears. They were going to go home, as least for a little while. They skipped towards the trail as their families headed out from the acorn camp.

However, their joy was short lived. As they approached the Place of River Turtles, none of the familiar sounds of daily life could be heard. All was eerily quiet. And as they stepped into the village area, there were no signs of life: no smoke rising from cooking fires, no children playing hoop-and-pole.

The place was a ghost town. Several of the Tule reed homes had collapsed. The only movement seemed to be a few small wild animals scurrying about looking for food.

Then a figure from the far end of the village approached Kilik's group. It was an old Chumash man. When he came closer, Kilik saw that it was one of the Council of Twelve. Nothing but skin and bones, he looked worse than the Indians at the mission.

"This is what we wanted you to see," Captain Castigar said smugly in Spanish. "There is nothing left of your home. You have nothing to go back to."

As Kilik and the others began to realize this truth, the old man came close enough to be heard. He, of course, only spoke and understood Chumash.

"I don't know what that man said to you, but men who looked just like him rode in here on their beasts and started rounding up our people," the old man said weakly. "Some escaped and ran off who knows where. The captured ones were dragged off, leaving only my wife and I and a couple of other old people. I guess we are too old and weak to be of any use, so they didn't bother with us."

He coughed and wheezed a few times before continuing.

"With no one to help us hunt or collect food, we slowly starved. Now I'm the only one left." He coughed again. "I'm not long for this world, myself."

"Where have the rest of our people been taken?" Solomol asked the captain of the guard in Spanish. "None of them were brought to the mission where we are."

"Other missions need workers, too," the captain replied. "Your people are probably scattered up and down these lands."

Kilik and his people were heart broken. Their home no longer existed. Their place in the Middle World had disappeared. And the rest of the Chumash people had been scattered to the four directions.

The old man stepped closer to Solomol and Salapay who stood close to one another and spoke to them in almost a whisper.

"They say there's a place across the northern mountain range where our people have gone," he said. "They've joined others who have escaped the strangers' work camps."

"Do you know where this is?" Solomol asked. "Is it far?"

The old man looked at Captain Castigar suspiciously.

"Are you sure he can't understand us?" the elder asked.

"Not a word," Salapay confirmed. "He thinks our language is worthless."

"Good. The place is near the base of Sacred Mountain," the old man said. "But the strangers watch the main trails looking for runaways. So you have to take the old animal paths to get there."

"Enough of this gibberish talk from an old man," the head of the guard bellowed. "Time to move on. Back to the mission now, all of you."

They bid a sad farewell to the man who was once a respected leader, the last survivor of the Place of River Turtles. The soldiers hurried the heart-broken people along, wanting to get back to the mission and their comfortable quarters as soon as possible.

But Kilik lingered a moment longer.

"What are you doing, son?" Solomol asked. "You'll get hit up side the head of you don't move along."

"I want to take one last look at the place we used to call home," Kilik replied. "I want to remember who I am and where I come from like you told me to, Father."

Chapter 10 - Is All Hope Lost?

During the walk back to the mission no one spoke. The joy of the day had vaporized, along with their hopes of ever going back to the life they once knew and loved.

More days of tedium and torture followed. The blur of days fogged Kilik and Tuhuy's minds as they lost track of time. Were their lives in the Place of River Turtles just dreams? Had they imagined those wonderful days of childhood in the natural world? It certainly seemed so.

The priests and soldiers marked the passage of time in very different ways than the

Chumash did. There were the days each month set aside to honor and pray to dead people called saints. And there was a list of other days: Advent, Ash Wednesday, Easter, Day of Ascension and Pentecost. These days had to be memorized by the Natives, along with the yearly calendar that had come from Spain.

None of these days coincided with the honored and respected days celebrated by the Chumash and other Natives. Winter Solstice, Summer Solstice, the beginning of Spring, Hutash. These ceremony days followed the cycles of Mother Earth and the Sky People, the sun, moon and stars.

But, however you marked the passage of time, it dragged by slowly with the drudgery of everyday life in the mission. With that passage of time, all the buildings that made up the mission were completed. Every adobe brick was made and placed by an Indian laborer. Every drop of white, limestone-based paint was applied to the walls by Indian hands. And with the completion of the bell tower, the bells were moved from the tree branches from which they hung. Hoisted using both Indian and animal labor, the bells were secured to their places in the tower.

Now the daily, weekly and monthly cycles of time kept by the priests could be proclaimed louder and further than ever before. Each time the bells tolled, they shouted out victory for the strangers. Victory for the priests and soldiers. Victory for the uninvited. Victory for the coyote-men.

But secretly the Chumash astronomers and ceremonial leaders continued to mark the traditional cycles of time in the old way. In order to prevent punishment, they learned to keep these things hidden and practiced far from priestly eyes.

One year, and then two, passed in captivity. Kilik and Tuhuy grew in size and strength, in spite of poor food and hard labor. The boys, now young teens, managed to lift one another's spirits when depression threatened to set in. And they made games out of their labors whenever possible–whenever they weren't being watched too closely.

Unfortunately, other Native laborers didn't fare as well. Harsh working conditions, physical punishment, injuries and diseases brought from Europe all took their toll on the people. Deaths of loved ones and friends mounted. Most of those who died were unceremoniously placed in unmarked graves. Of course, a padre marked down the name of the deceased and the date of his death in a big book, but that was all. In the minds of the priests, this was another soul harvested for heaven. Otherwise, these departed Indians were gone and forgotten by the Spaniards.

But the loss of each laborer created the need for another to take his place. For, even though construction of the mission had been completed, there were plenty of other daily tasks that needed tending to. Fields had to be plowed. Crops had to be planted and watered. Cattle had to be fed, slaughtered and prepared as either food or leather. Saddles and other leather goods needed to be created or repaired.

So, more Natives had to be rounded up and herded to the mission. New recruits had to be converted and taught. The pattern had to be repeated day in and day out--year in and year out.

Faced with such overwhelming challenges and tragedy, many Natives simply gave up. Suffering from fatigue, disease and an overall sense of defeat, they accepted the teachings of the strangers. They accepted that their ancient traditions must give way to the power of the priests, the commands of the guards. After all, for those who believed, the black book promised a life of rest and peace at the end of this life of torment and struggle.

But through it all, Solomol and Salapay continued to repeat their silent vows. Some how, some way, some day, they would be free. Or at least their children would be.

Chapter 11 - News Spreads

From time to time a Spanish expedition would come to the mission bringing much needed supplies, mail from mission headquarters in Mexico City, and news from other missions in California. A few days later the expedition would move on to another of the missions , presidios or towns scattered across this province of the Spanish empire. They left each mission carrying the hides, grains and other products for export produced by the mission Indians.

One such expedition arrived on a warm day with alarming news from nearby missions.

Indians at the Mission Santa Barbara had risen up in rebellion against their captors and temporarily seized control of that outpost. Indian runners from that mission carried details of the revolt to another neighboring mission, and they too rose up in rebellion. Both rebellions, however, had been squelched within a matter of days.

News of these revolts was only shared in secret with the priests and soldiers at Kilik's mission. The Spaniards didn't want this news to embolden their Indians into thinking they could follow the example of the Indians of Santa Barbara.

However, Kilik was cleaning up Father Espíritu's room and accidentally overheard the news as the expedition captain reported it in the shared living space within the padres' quarters. As the teenager dusted the shelves in his master's room, the captain recounted the events of the conflict with a great deal of urgency.

Kilik quit his dusting and crept quietly to the door that separated him from the men in the next room. With his ear less than an inch from the door's flimsy wood, he strained to hear what was said.

"Keep a watchful eye out for any unfamiliar Indians arriving here," the expedition captain said. "They will most likely be bringing news of the revolt to your Indians. They may also bring with them ideas on how your Indians could take over this mission."

"We have already quelled a major escape attempt here," Father Fiero replied. "These Indians know too well the wrath of God delivered by the hands of our own trustees and soldiers. I don't think they'd dare try anything so bold as rebellion."

"I wouldn't be too sure," the expedition captain responded. "We promised these Indians that they'd be free to return to their villages one day after becoming Christians and learning the new skills we've taught. Many of them have figured out that the only way they're really getting out of here is when their spirits escape their dying flesh. I believe they've taken all they're going to take."

Just then Tuhuy returned to the Father Espíritu's room after finishing a chore for the priest. As he opened the outer door, the hinges squeaked. Kilik immediately knew that the men in the other room heard that squeak. Without hesitation, the boy sprang into action.

"Are you sure no heathen ears can hear our conversation?" the expedition captain asked from the other room.

Captain Castigar, who stood near Father Fiero, rushed to the door to Father Espíritu's room. Quickly swinging it open, he looked to see who might be standing behind it listening. To his surprise, no one was there. He immediately searched every corner of the room, under the priest's cot, and inside the wooden wardrobe that stood along one wall. He raced out the room's second door that led into the mission's courtyard and scanned the area. He saw no one and stepped back inside.

"It must've been the wind," he reported to the men. "Nothing to worry about."

What neither Castigar nor the others knew was that several days earlier Kilik had discovered an outside storage bin near Father Espíritu's room. The bin usually held firewood, but was empty at the moment, waiting to be refilled with a fresh supply. When Kilik heard the hinges squeak as Tuhuy entered the room, he had to act fast. Pushing his cousin ahead of him, he immediately rushed to the empty bin, and both boys dove in, closing the lid behind them. They just barely missed being seen by Castigar.

When they were sure the coast was clear, the cousins climbed out of the bin. They walked quickly out to the fields where their fathers were working. Fearing discovery by one of the turtle-men, Kilik rapidly explained what he'd heard in the padres' living room.

"You did good," Solomol told his son. "This is important news. Now go back to your chores and act as if you heard nothing. Salapay and I will call a meeting of our trusted allies here at the mission."

"Father, be careful," Tuhuy said to Salapay. "We couldn't bear to watch you receive another flogging."

"Don't worry," he replied. "We learned our lesson about secret spies. Even the walls of the mission buildings seem to have ears. Now go."

Seeing an approaching soldier, the two men returned to their labors as their sons walked calmly back towards the padres' quarters.

That night the Chumash men gathered in secret to discuss news of the revolts.

Some felt it was time they took action as well. Others believed it was too risky to even try. Solomol had lost all patience with those unwilling to take a chance.

"How much longer are you willing to stand by and watch our people work themselves to death?" he asked the men around him. "How much longer are you going to do nothing as our infants and elders fall ill and wither away? As for me, I am no longer willing to wait. I say its time to fight for our freedom or die, if we must, fighting for our children's freedom!"

That seemed to motivate most of the men to rally for the cause. Salapay called for a show of hands: which men chose to fight, and which ones declined. Those who decided not to participate were asked to leave. That left a handful of men committed to fighting. At Salapay's request, each man pledged to come up with ideas to help them devise a plan of attack. They would have to act soon, they all agreed.

Chapter 12 - The Countdown Begins

A few Indians always traveled with the expeditions to do most of the manual labor: loading and unloading the pack animals, carrying equipment or supplies that didn't fit on the pack animals and taking care of tasks demanded by the traveling priests.

These Indians stayed in the single men's quarters and ate meals with the local mission Indians during their stay. What the priests and soldiers didn't know was that these Natives secretly carried messages to and from the Indians in the various missions.

That night Salapay and Solomol called a meeting of their allies to hear what the visiting Natives had to say. They met under cover of darkness near a large oak tree a few hundred yards south of the mission walls. This time Kilik and Tuhuy were allowed to take part.

"My son here overheard the padres talking about revolts at the other missions," Solomol reported. "What details can you give us?"

"Those rebellions were defeated rather quickly," said Mateo, the spokesman for the visiting Indians. "They were not very well organized or equipped, but they <u>have</u> inspired others to take action."

"We are more than ready to free ourselves from these cruel captors," Salapay said. "But we can't do it alone."

"Many Indians have escaped to the mountains and are preparing an attack," Mateo replied. "This mission will be their first target, because it is closest to their hideout."

"That's great news," Solomol said. "When do they plan to attack? What signal will they use to warn us?"

"The attack will begin in one week, on the first day of Summer Solstice," Mateo whispered. "In the early morning hours of the longest day of sunlight, when Grandfather Sun's powers are strongest—we surround the mission. Then we move in during the soldiers' breakfast."

"Perfect," Solomol said. "What do we do?"

"While the soldiers are having breakfast, sneak into their storage room and remove as many weapons as you can. Hide them somewhere so they can't be used against our warriors. Then wait for our signal, the call of the owl."

The plan was laid out and discussed so that all the Native men and boys knew what to expect. Then everyone started to quietly return to his quarters. However, Solomol and Salapay stayed behind to speak to their sons.

While Kilik was extremely excited about the plans, Tuhuy, on the other hand, was more worried than anything.

"Many of our people will die when the soldiers begin firing their rifles," he said. "Our arrows and spears are no match for their bullets."

"Many of our people have already died a slow and painful death at their hands," Kilik replied. "I'd rather die fighting for my freedom than to spend another agonizing day in this place."

"I'm glad to hear you speak words of courage," Solomol told his son. "But you won't be fighting <u>or</u> dying when this battle begins."

"What? Then why have you included us in this plan?" Kilik asked. "You don't think I'm capable of fighting?"

"Remember what I told you before?" Solomol said. "Salapay and I expect the two of you to work together and stay with the children when the fighting starts. Keep them out of harm's way."

"But--"

"But nothing," Solomol said firmly. "If this rebellion fails, our only hope for the future of our people is the younger generation. So your successful escape is our reason for fighting. Got that?"

Kilik took in a deep breath and blew it out. "Got it," he said.

"Good," Kilik's father and uncle said together. "When the owl signal is given, go to the chapel and wait inside. Don't come out for any reason until one of us comes to get you. Agreed?

"Agreed," the boys repeated again.

With that the fathers headed back to their quarters while the sons headed for theirs.

The following morning the expedition loaded up and left the mission. Watching them go, Salapay and Solomol knew the countdown had begun. Ready or not, in one week they'd make a stand that could decide the fate of the inland Chumash Nation.

The Natives that knew of the plan slept uneasy all week. During the day, they watched the soldiers, looking for any sign that they knew of the plan–any change of routine, addition of manpower or arrival of new weapons. All seemed quiet.

As they continued to work with Father Espíritu, Kilik and Tuhuy kept their ears open for any signs that the padres expected trouble. The boys heard nothing. However, Father Espíritu seemed to become especially attentive to the needs of the Natives at the mission. He went out of his way to bring leftover food from the padre's kitchen to Kilik and Tuhuy. The masters of the mission were always fed the most flavorful foods.

And the compassionate padre also brought a few medical supplies he'd managed to "borrow" from the mission's medicine cabinet. He secretly passed these along to the boys for them to take back to Indian families to keep in case they needed treatments.

Then on Thursday of that week, the father gave the boys a burlap bundle to take with them.

"You'll need this tomorrow, but don't open it until you get back to your quarters," he said. "I don't want the soldiers to become suspicious of what's inside."

The boys didn't know what to make of this sudden show of generosity and asked the padre what prompted these gifts.

"Let's just say I'm not fond of the way the missions treat you Indians," Father Espíritu said. "Nowhere in the scriptures are we told to enslave non-believers, force them to convert and do back breaking work for us. It just isn't right."

The boys gratefully took the sack from the padre and returned to their quarters using a route that didn't take them directly across the open plaza. Once inside the boys' dorm, they set the sack on the floor between their mats. Tuhuy kept a lookout to make sure no one watched while Kilik peered inside.

There he found a bundle of dried meat, a couple of loaves of bread, a container of pine nuts and chia seeds, along with a few other food items.

"Why would the padre send us a bag of food?" Kilik wondered out loud. Taking a quick peek at the bag's contents, Tuhuy said, "That's traveling food. Does Father Espíritu know what's coming?"

Puzzled, the boys decided to hide their prize out of sight in the middle of a large bush that grew just outside their dorm. They'd have to talk to their fathers later about what this meant.

Chapter 13 - Summer Solstice

The following day, the Summer Solstice sun began its journey across the sky in the usual way. Nocturnal creatures found shady places where they'd rest and spend the daylight hours. The plants, insects and four-legged inhabitants of the Middle World awoke as the sun's warmth stirred them.

Within the mission, the first morning bell sounded as it had done for the countless days the people of the Place of River Turtles had lived there. Roosters crowed. Donkeys brayed. Cattle grazed.

In a short while, the bells rang out again,

announcing the time for breakfast. Nervously, the two cousins headed for the food line where another serving of tasteless mush awaited them. Wonono steered Stuk over to where Kilik waited for his food, instructing her to stay close to her brother.

"Listen to your brother and do exactly what he says," Wonono said.

"Why do I-"

"Now is not the time, young lady," her mother interrupted in a stern tone. "Dangerous things are about to take place, and your brother is in charge of you until further notice."

Stuk fell silent. She'd never heard her mother say anything like that. Never.

Kilik and Tuhuy watched as their fathers quietly slipped away from their place in the food line. A few other Native men did the same, each heading in a different direction than the others. They would rendezvous behind the soldiers' storage room and wait until the coast was clear.

Soon all the soldiers left their quarters and headed for their dining room. Once the Spaniards had stepped inside to eat, Solomol signaled his small band of Native men. They rushed into the soldiers' quarters where they found Reynaldo relaxing on a cot in the corner. He was left to guard the place while the soldier's were away.

"Reynaldo, what a surprise," Salapay said. "Take him, gag him and tie him to the cot," he told the other men. Remembering that it was Reynaldo who had spied on them and reported their plans to the Spaniards, the Chumash men were more than happy to do so. Using cloth and ropes found nearby, the Natives gagged and tied up the very surprised trustee.

Once that was accomplished, the men lifted the key to the storage door from its hook inside the soldiers' quarters. Again, making sure that no one was watching, Salapay inserted the key and opened the lock that secured the storage room door. Now, moving as quickly as possible, the Native men grabbed as many rifles and swords as they could carry and headed for the woods beyond the mission walls.

As they stepped outside the walls, they encountered a group of Native warriors that were waiting for the signal to charge into the mission. These men carried extra bows, arrows and spears, which they offered to Solomol, Salapay and the others.

Seeing that Solomol's men had carried out their part of the plan, the head of the troop of warriors gave the signal to attack: three owl hoots. Seconds later, the circle of warriors surrounding the mission stood up and released in unison a blood-curdling war cry.

Climbing walls and storming through gates, the Native army charged into the mission compound. Their plan was to capture all of the priests and soldiers, relieve them of their weapons and lock them inside the priest's quarters.

Meanwhile, eating breakfast halfway across the mission grounds with the other Indian laborers, Kilik heard the war cry go up. "Let's go!" he told Stuk and Tuhuy. "To the chapel!"

They scurried toward the chapel where they were surprised to find Father Espíritu waiting at the massive wooden doors. The kids froze, worried the padre might report their unusual movement to Father Fiero. However, using a key that hung from his neck, he instead unlocked the doors and flung them open.

"Get inside quickly," he said in a loud whisper. "I'll gather up the rest of the children and be right back."

The padre was gone before Kilik could say or do anything. He and the others stepped inside, closing, but not locking, the doors behind them.

Upon hearing the war cry, the soldiers had immediately abandoned their breakfasts.

A few rushed to the weapons storage room while others headed for their sleeping quarters. Finding the storage unit open, a half-dozen turtle-men stepped inside.

"Our spare rifles, swords and ammunition have been stolen!" one of the men reported to Captain Castigar. "But they didn't find our hidden stash of weapons."

"So, our own Indians are in on this!" he replied. "They'll pay dearly when this is over."

Just then a line of warriors carrying spears and bows came running toward the captain and his men.

"Retreat to the weapons room!" the captain shouted. "Set up a barricade and prepare to repel the attack!" The men moved quickly just as the first volley of arrows flew into their midst, wounding two soldiers.

Using war shields to protect themselves, the rest of the soldiers returned from the soldiers' quarters with Reynaldo in tow.

"We found Reynaldo bound and gagged in our quarters," one of the soldiers reported.

Addressing the Indian trustee, Castiar said, "Mount a horse and ride like the wind to the presidio at the nearest mission. Tell them to send as many soldiers as possible to quell another uprising."

"But señor, a man could get killed doing that," Reynaldo protested.

"I promise you that a man will get killed if he doesn't," Castigar replied, pointing his pistol at the trustee's head.

"Yes, sir, right away, sir," Reynaldo said, and he stood to leave.

"All right, men, load your rifles and prepare your swords," the captain commanded. "Take no prisoners!"

At the chapel, Kilik and the others heard more war cries in the distance followed by several shots from the soldiers' pistols. Then Father Espíritu entered the sanctuary leading a group of Native youth of different ages.

"Father, why are you doing this?" Kilik asked when all the children were safely inside.

"I told you, my son," the padre said. "I don't agree with the church's treatment of the Native people. These methods are being used in missions all over the Americas. It's got to stop."

"And how did you know we'd be needing that bag of food you gave us?" Tuhuy asked.

"You're not the only one who listens in on other people's conversations," the priest answered with a smile. "Now I must join the other padres behind closed doors and pretend I didn't know anything about this rebellion. Keep the chapel doors closed until things quiet down."

Father Espíritu closed the door as he exited the chapel, leaving about a dozen fearful Native children inside. All they could do was hope, pray and wait.

——

Chapter 14 - A Near Miss

Outside the chapel, a stand-off between the Spanish soldiers and the Native warriors was developing. The soldiers had enough weapons and ammunition to prevent the Indians from charging into the storage room. The warriors had enough arrows and spears to prevent the soldiers from escaping their enclosure. The armed Natives hid behind low walls within the mission compound or peered around corners of buildings near the storeroom. And waited.

Inside the chapel, many of the children were growing hungry and even more fearful.

Where were their parents? What was happening to them? The younger ones, including Stuk, began to whine and cry.

"I'm hungry and thirsty," Stuk complained. "When will they bring us some food?" She looked at her brother with a furrowed brow and said, "Don't just sit there. Why don't you do something? Do something."

That's when Kilik remembered that his father had put him in charge of the children. Now he knew what that meant. It meant that, for the time being, he and Tuhuy had to feed them and protect them.

"All right, Kimi," the boy said. "I <u>will</u> do something." Turning to his cousin, Kilik said, "Tuhuy, you stay here, guard the children and keep them quiet. I'll go retrieve that sack of food we hid."

"But you could get shot or something," Tuhuy protested.

"Listen," Kilik replied. "Just be quiet and listen for a minute."

Both boys turned their attention to what was going on outside. Things were actually very quiet at the moment.

"The fighting has died down, so I think I can get to the food bag and get back without any problem," the older cousin said.

"Okay, but be careful," Tuhuy replied. "I don't want to have to watch these children by myself." Then to the children, he quietly announced, "Kilik is going to get some food. The rest of us will stay here and stay quiet so the soldiers don't find us."

The children quieted down and indicated they understood. Kilik slowly opened and peered out the chapel door. He saw no movement outside. Carefully he opened the door just far enough to slip out and then quietly closed it behind him.

Staying close to the buildings for cover, the boy moved cautiously toward the young men's dorm. On his way, he passed other Indians who either were armed and waiting to attack the soldiers or were laborers just trying to stay out of danger.

The storeroom where the soldiers had positioned themselves had small windows along one outer wall. A soldier had taken up a position looking out each of those windows. He could easily target and kill anyone who came into view. That angle kept the Native warriors from being able to sneak up on the Spaniards from behind. It also kept other Indians from moving about the mission grounds much.

Near the soldiers' storeroom Kilik saw several dead Native men lying on the ground. They'd been shot by the soldiers. Kilik suddenly and frantically realized that his father or uncle might lie among those bodies.

From behind a bush, the boy strained to see their faces, but he was too far away to see them all.

Quickly Kilik continued on his journey and found the sack of food. And just as quickly he turned back towards the chapel. On the way he decided to take a short cut across the mission courtyard, which was an open area with a fountain in the middle. As he moved a shot rang out from the storehouse, immediately followed by the "thwack" of a bullet striking an adobe wall close behind Kilik. A near miss!

His heart pounding, the teen leapt behind the sidewall of the fountain. Seeing what had happened, a warrior hiding nearby shot an arrow toward the window the bullet had come from. This forced the soldier inside to duck, allowing Kilik time to run the rest of the way across the plaza. He raced to the chapel, pausing at the door to catch his breath.

Once inside, he and Tuhuy divided up

the food and passed it out to the others. Kilik decided not to mention what had just happened because he didn't want to alarm his cousin.

"You know this is really just enough food for one day," Tuhuy said when they'd finished distributing the food. "We'll need to go out and find more."

"We also need to find out if our parents are all right," Kilik said. "A few Natives have been killed by the soldiers, but I couldn't see if our fathers were among them." Tuhuy hadn't even thought of that possibility and was now shaken by the realization.

Just then the chapel door opened and both their fathers entered. What a joyous reunion for both fathers and sons that was. Each of the men also carried additional burlap bags of food, which they presented to their sons.

"The soldiers are barricaded in the supply storeroom and are shooting at anyone who comes into view," Solomol said. "Keep everyone inside."

"You'll get no argument from anyone here," Kilik replied without revealing his close call.

"We don't know how long this stand-off will last, but we're planning on rushing the soldiers after dark," Salapay said. "We'll figure out what to do next when that's over."

What none of the Natives knew was that Reynaldo had been successful in mounting a horse and leaving the mission early that morning. He rode non-stop to the closest presidio to report the Native revolt. Upon hearing the news, two-dozen soldiers had quickly armed themselves and set out at full speed. By late afternoon they were well on their way to quell the rebellion.

Just as the Native warriors had done at dawn that morning, the new troops surrounded the mission and approached quietly at sunset. They, too, planned to attack under cover of darkness. And as the Native warriors were just about to begin their fresh attack on the storeroom, the newly arrived batch of soldiers launched their attack of the warriors.

Inside the chapel, Kilik and Tuhuy heard the eruption of gunfire. Peeking out the chapel door, Kilik saw the flashes of light that shot from the rifle muzzles of the soldiers. He heard the wails of warriors as some of the bullets hit their marks. Quickly the teen shut the door.

"It looks like a fresh supply of soldiers has arrived from one of the other missions," Kilik reported to Tuhuy. "They have our warriors pinned down, caught in crossfire from soldiers inside the storeroom as well as the soldiers attacking from outside the mission."

"That doesn't sound good," Tuhuy said in a worried voice. "What are we going to do?"

"We need to rig up a way to lock the chapel doors from the inside so the soldiers can't get to us," Kilik suggested.

He and Tuhuy studied the interior door handles for a moment. There was one vertical iron handle on each door. Tuhuy saw that there was an open space between each handle and the door. Suddenly it came to him. He knew what he needed to solve the problem.

Searching the chapel quickly, he found a long metal candlestick holder standing near the altar. It was just about the right size, Tuhuy thought. He thrust the round object through the two handle openings creating a simple crossbar lock.

"Great idea," Kilik exclaimed. "Nobody can get in now. We just need to keep quiet so the soldiers will think there's no one in here."

At that moment the boys heard a rustling noise coming from behind the chapel's altar. It sounded like someone had found another way to get in!

Chapter 15 - Call of Duty

"We have to do something," Kilik said instinctively. "We can't let the soldiers get to the children." Quickly scanning his immediate surroundings, he located a wooden chair against the back wall. He picked it up and ran toward the altar fully expecting to bring the chair down on the head of an invading soldier.

Just as he reached the altar, Kilik saw a man emerge from a trap door in the floor behind the altar. The boy lifted the heavy chair over his head. Then, before he could thrust the chair toward the intruder, he saw that it was his own father. In a state of shock, Kilik dropped the chair behind him. It broke into pieces as it hit the floor with a crash.

"Son, are you all right?" Solomol asked, startled by the noise.

With great relief, Kilik rushed to his father, engulfing him in a powerful embrace.

"I thought you were a soldier coming to harm us," Kilik said with a gasp. Then pulling back, he asked. "How did you get in?"

Pointing to the trap door, Solomol replied, "As one of the builders of this chapel I knew there was a hidden back door into this place. It was too risky to come in from the front. Bullets are flying everywhere."

Seeing that it was his uncle and not an intruding soldier, Tuhuy came up behind his cousin and asked, "What about my father? Is he all right?"

"You can ask him yourself," Solomol said. "He's right here."

The boys looked down to see Salapay

hobbling up the steps from below the trap door. His leg was bandaged.

"Father, what happened?" Tuhuy asked.

"One of Captain Castigar's bullets nicked the side of my leg," Salapay replied. "It's nothing, really."

Tuhuy hugged his father, saying almost tearfully, "I'm afraid we're all going to die, and I'm <u>not</u> afraid to admit it."

"What do we do now?" Kilik asked, looking from his father to his uncle.

Solomol put both his hands on his son's shoulders and said, "The time has come."

"What?" Kilik asked. "What do you mean?"

"Its time for you to take all that Salapay and I have taught you and put that knowledge and those skills to use," his father said solemnly. "Time to call on the courage we talked about. Time to take your place as a man and a leader."

"What are you saying, Father?"

"With Tuhuy's help, you must take all the children and escape from this place," Solomol said. "The mission is engulfed in chaos and confusion."

"But what about you and mother, Uncle Salapay and Auntie Yol? What about the other Chumash people here?"

"We have to stay and take our chances here," Salapay said. "If all the Indians here try to escape, it will be slow going. It will be easier for the soldiers to come after us and track us down. If you children slip away, they may not notice or care."

"But where will we go?" Kilik asked. "There's nothing left at our village. They'd just round us up and bring us back from there anyway."

"Remember what our elder said when we visited the Place of River Turtles?" his father replied. "He said it so the soldiers couldn't understand."

"I remember," Kilik answered. "He said there's a village where Natives who've escaped from the missions and their soldiers have gone to live. But I don't know how to get there."

"But you do. You and I were halfway there the day you killed your first deer."

Kilik thought back to that day, remembering the directions and the landmarks his father had shown him.

"At dawn, just before sunrise, I look to the east, to Morning Star," he said. "I head straight for her until I come to the Mother Oak."

"That's right," Solomol said excitedly. "You do remember. But stay off the main trails as you travel. More soldiers might be coming that way. After reaching Mother Oak, where do you go?"

"I head north on the Path Made by Deer until I come to the old hunting camp," he continued. "But where do I go from there?

"Think back," his father said. "You could

see Shrine Mountain from the hill near that camp. Remember?"

Kilik pictured the view from that hill.

"Yes, I do," he said.

"So, from the hunting camp, you head for Shrine Mountain," Solomol instructed. "Then, from the top of that grassy mountain, you scan the horizon to the north and east. The tallest mountain you see in that direction is Sacred Mountain."

"That's where the village of runaways is," Kilik said excitedly. "That's what the elder told us." Then Kilik had another thought. "But what about food for the journey?"

"You've made your first kill," Kilik's father reminded him. "You are a trained and skilled hunter."

He stepped back down into the space under the trap door. When he came back up he was carrying a bow and quiver of arrows.

"One of the Native warriors brought these to use against the soldiers, but I'm giving them to you," he added.

He handed weapons to Kilik as another thought crossed the boy's mind. "What about you and mother and the others? Will we ever see you again?"

"What does Kilik mean will we ever see you again?" Stuk asked as she approached the altar area. "What's going on?"

Solomol knelt down so he could talk to his daughter at her level. He smiled.

"What's going on is that you get to go on an adventure with Kilik, Tuhuy and the other children," Solomol said cheerily. "And you need to continue listening to your brother and doing as he says."

"Why does he always get to be in charge?" the little girl asked. "When will it be my turn? My turn?"

"Ladybug, you'll be in charge of helping to find food for the children on your journey. How's that? You helped your mother find food many times."

"That's right," she said with satisfaction. "So, when we will see you and mother again?"

"Soon, Ladybug. Soon. We'll join you just as quickly as we can."

Just then, war cries could be heard from outside, followed by a volley of gunfire. Sounds of the battle grew louder as the fighting seemed to move closer to the chapel.

"We must join the fight again," Solomol said as he stood up. "We have to keep the soldiers from retaking the mission at least until morning after all of you escape."

Out in the mission compound, a loud explosion cut through the night, followed by screams of pain.

"We're out of time," Kilk's father said hurriedly. "Your mother sends her love to you both." Then he whispered into his son's ear. "Whether I see you again in this life or in the Spirit World, I will send my Spirit Helpers to guide you."

Kilik's eyes began to well up with tears, but he breathed deeply and held them back. He couldn't allow the others to see him in a weak moment.

Kilik and Stuk hugged their father with all their might. Tuhuy did the same with his father.

"Wait here in the chapel until dawn," Solomol instructed as they ended their embrace. "Then use this passage way to get out of the chapel. It leads to the secret door we built at the back wall of the mission. You won't be seen as you head eastward down the hill."

With those words, Solomol and Salapay scrambled back down through the trap door and into the night.

Kilik was immediately filled with feelings of fear, dread and uncertainty. They washed over him like a flood until he thought he would drown. Then, from somewhere deep within his mind, Kilik heard his father's voice speak to him as he'd done on the day of his first hunt.

"Courage comes from within you by joining your mind to your heart," Solomol's voice said. "If you love and respect those who need your protection, the courage you need will rise up in spite of any fear you feel."

Focusing on those words and the strength he felt the day of that hunt, Kilik could sense an inner strength rising up within him. A sense of determination rose up along with it. He turned and looked at Tuhuy, Stuk and the Native children there in the chapel.

He began to feel a strong sense of duty to protect them. His father's words echoed in his mind again. "The courage you need will rise up in spite of any fear you feel."

And there it was, just has his father had said, that feeling of courage he needed.

Chapter 16 - The Final Escape

Kilik convinced his sister and the others that they needed to get some rest before beginning their journey in the morning. The hard, wooden pews in the chapel made terrible beds but it was all they had.

Kilik's sleep was disturbed by nightmares of being caught by the soldiers along the trail and getting lost before reaching Sacred Mountain. Each time he awoke from the nightmare, he made a vow not to allow these things to happen. Dreams, he'd learned from his elders, often pointed out things you should take care of so you can prevent them from happening in real life.

Just before dawn, the soft cooing of mourning doves filtered into Kilik's mind from somewhere outside. He awoke and immediately realized it was time for his little troop to depart. Quickly he ran from pew to pew and awakened those who would be his traveling companions.

He put Tuhuy and Stuk in charge of their food bags and reminded everyone to remain very quiet. Then he led the way down through the trap door and out the back of the chapel.

Walking single-file, the line of children made their way into the woods beyond the mission grounds. Heading east, they threaded their way through the underbrush that grew thickly in the area. Soon they came to a little hill that gave Kilik a clear view of the eastern sky. There, hanging low above the horizon was Morning Star, shining like a beacon of freedom.

"See that star just above the horizon," Kilik said to the others. "She is Morning Star, and she will be our first guide on this journey. She will light our way until Grandfather Sun wakes up."

Each child said a greeting to the star before continuing their trip. Soon, the sun rose to brightly expose the rolling hills around them. Kilik realized it was time to move deeper into the tall grass and wooded areas.

"Why can't we just stay on the trail?" Stuk complained. "This tall grass is hard to walk through, and my legs are beginning to hurt. Beginning to hurt."

"Kimi, your brother is in charge of getting us safely to our destination," Tuhuy responded. "Do you want the soldiers to find us and drag us back to the mission?"

"No-o-o-o," she said in a long, low tone that signaled she understood their situation. "But can we stop and eat? I'm hungry."

"Of course," her brother replied. "Let's sit under that tree."

He pointed to a large oak that provided good shade.

After a quick break, their journey continued in that pattern for the rest of the morning. They moved more slowly than Kilik and his father had moved on their hunting trip because this troop of children were not experienced in long distance travel.

At mid-day they reached Mother Oak, the first turning point in their journey. During the morning, dark clouds had moved across the sky and parked themselves over Chumash territory. Now they seemed to be ready to release the moisture they held. Soon small drops began to fall.

Kilik decided it was time for another rest. He was careful not to stop too close to the great oak because it grew right beside the main trail. He located the northward Path Made by Deer and headed in that direction.

Along that path, he found a stand of short grass surrounded by shrubs that prevented anyone on the main trail or at the big tree from seeing them.

They munched quietly on their trail meal as a faint sound reached their ears. Listening closely, Kilik realized it was the sound of horse hooves. As the pounding sound grew louder and louder, Kilik knew that a group of soldiers was riding on the trail.

"Everyone quickly lay flat on the ground and don't move or make a sound," he whispered. Sensing the real danger, everyone did as they were told. For long minutes, the children held still as it became obvious the soldiers were also taking a break. From the noises he heard, Kilik could tell they were dismounting under the Mother Tree. Using hand signals, he motioned for the scared children to quietly follow him and do as he did.

Crawling slowly across the grass, Kilik moved further away from Mother Oak. In a single-file line, the children did the same. Kilik made his way to the dirt deer path. At this point, the path began to wind its way through a grove of oak trees. Kilik knew they couldn't be seen from the great oak tree and signaled everyone to quietly stand up. As they stood, the group startled a flock of birds roosting in the branches of the trees.

The fleeing flock created a burst of noise that was heard by the soldiers. Suspicious that the birds may have been startled by runaway Indians, the soldiers moved on foot towards the area.

Meanwhile, Kilik feared that the soldiers would be coming, so he whispered loudly, "Run up this path as fast as you can without making any noise."

The kids again did as they were told,

running as fast as their bare feet could carry them. Kilik decided to take up the rear of the retreat so he could see if and when any soldiers followed.

Luckily for the young Natives, these soldiers were tired of hunting Indians and soon returned to their horses. Mounting up, they continued their journey eastward along the main trail.

Kilik caught up to rest of his group who had grown tired and stopped to rest in the midst of some bushes beside the path. They were all panting from the run, and he signaled for them to be quiet again so he could listen for the soldiers. When nothing further was heard from that direction, he sighed a big sigh of relief. Everyone else did the same.

"That was a close one," Tuhuy said. "I have to say, Kilik, that your skills as a hunter, and even a warrior, amaze me."

"Don't praise my abilities until <u>after</u> we get safely to the village at Sacred Mountain," Kilik replied. "We're not out of danger yet."

"I'm just saying that you're the right man for the job," his cousin said. "And I do mean man."

Kilik blushed a little at Tuhuy's comment as a gentle rain began to fall on them.

"We'd better get going so we can make it to the old hunting camp before dark," Kilik suggested. "We can get out of the rain there."

Kilik led the way northward on the Path Made by Deer. It wasn't long before they reached the camp but found it in rather sad shape. No Natives had used it in a long time. Even though it was still raining, Kilik had everyone pitch in to repair the camp's shelters. Drawing on skills learned from his father and uncle, Kilik began teaching the others how to use natural vines to tie branches together. These were lashed across the top of shelter frames that still stood in place.

Fortunately, the camp included a still-intact, covered area where firewood and dry kindling had long ago been stored. Again, using a traditional technique learned from Salapay, Kilik got a fire going that was protected from the rain by long branches stretching out from nearby trees. The fire burned into the night as the exhausted escapees fell asleep under shelters built by their ancestors.

The following morning the travelers awoke to a grey sky, which was visible through the leaves of the tall surrounding trees. After finishing off the last of their traveling food, the courageous crew headed northward for Shrine Mountain.

"Why is it called Shrine Mountain?" Stuk asked as they walked.

"Because it is the place we Chumash have erected prayer poles and built shrine offerings since the beginning of time," Tuhuy answered, repeating what his elders had taught him. "From the treeless peak of Shrine Mountain, the Sky People can easily hear our prayers and see our dedication to the old ways."

"And you can see Sacred Mountain from there," Kilik added. "That's the center of our Chumash world. It is the source of balance and power for us."

Soon the children left the wooded lowlands and reached the base of Shrine Mountain. "Father said we must climb to the top of this mountain in order to see the way to Sacred Mountain," Kilik said.

"Then to the top of the mountain we shall go," Tuhuy said in a cheery voice. "Right?"

A dozen young voices echoed, "Right!"

And off they went. As they slowly made their way up the grassy slope, the grey clouds were thinning and disappearing. Making several rest stops along the way, it was late morning before they reached the summit.

When they reached the top, the travelers came upon several prayer poles that had occupied the area for years–signs that generations of Chumash people had made their prayers upon this spiritual spot.

"We don't have any feathers or poles to put up," Tuhuy said. "But we could still stand upon this spiritual mountain and make our prayers."

"But don't you have to know the special ways to begin prayers?" one of the older children asked. "Aren't there certain things we have to say and do to make the prayers, right?"

Tuhuy thought for a moment, trying to form an appropriate reply.

"It's true that we haven't learned all there is to learn about our sacred traditions," Kilik said unexpectedly. "But we are the future of the Chumash people. We must do the best we can with what we know and what we have. It is up to us."

Tuhuy, usually the thinker of the pair, was thoroughly impressed by his cousin's words. So, each child took a turn expressing what was in his or her heart. All their fears and hopes were laid out on that mountaintop. The common thread winding its way through all their words was their concern about the future. Would they survive? Would they be all right? Would the people of the Place of River Turtles continue to live on?

As Tuhuy contemplated their unknown future, the last of the clouds faded from view. Looking southward over the lands of his ancestors, he saw a beautiful sight materialize before his eyes.

"Turn around," he said to his cousin.

Looking over his shoulder, Kilik found himself looking at a full rainbow arch across the sky. Everyone one turned to see.

"Grandmother Rainbow has heard us," Tuhuy said. "I believe she is telling us that everything is going to be all right."

Then, if that wasn't already enough, a second rainbow appeared above the first.

"It's a double rainbow," Kilik said. "All our troubles began after the double moon rings appeared in the night sky, foretelling of the coming of dangerous times. Now those times are ending, at least for us. Everything is going to be more than just all right. As long as we remember who we are and where we came from."

As the rainbows faded from view, the children headed for Sacred Mountain, singing an emotional song of hope and gratitude.

THE END

Afterward

Today, inland Chumash people continue to live in and around the Santa Ynez Valley. While living their busy modern lives, many members of the tribe are also busy relearning their language and culture. These things were stolen from them as the Spanish, Mexican and then American people moved onto the Chumash lands in wave after wave of immigrations.

You can learn more about contemporary Chumash people by contacting the Chumash Culture Department located at the tribe's headquarters in Santa Ynez, California. And you might find it interesting to know that today many Chumash parents are once again giving their children Chumash names similar to the names of the characters in this book.

Many of the descendants of other California Natives who suffered through and survived the historical mission period are also re-learning their languages and recapturing their cultures. Learn more by finding the tribes in your area and researching their histories, cultures and contemporary lives.

Bibliography of Research Sources

1. Castillo, Elias. <u>Cross of Thorns: The Enslavement of California's Indians by the Spanish Missions</u>. Craven Street Books, Fresno, 2015.

2. Fogel, Daniel. <u>Junipero Serra, the Vatican, and Enslavement Theology.</u>

3. Costo, Rupert and Jeannette, Ed. <u>The Missions of California: A Legacy of Genocide</u>.

4. Santa Barbara Museum of Natural History. <u>California's Chumash Indians</u>.

5. Richard Applegate and the Santa Ynez Chumash Education Committee. <u>Samala-English Dictionary: A Guide to the Samala Language of the Ineseño Chumash People</u>. 2007.

6. Jean Francois de la Perouse. <u>Life in a California Mission: The Journals of Jean Francois La Perouse</u>. Heyday, Berkeley. 1969

7. Deborah A. Miranda. <u>Bad Indians: A Tribal Memoir</u>. Heyday, Berkeley, CA. 2013.

8. John Johnson, PhD. ; Chumash Social Organization: An Ethnographic Perspective, University of California, Santa Barbara, 1988 (Doctoral Dissertation).

9. Blackburn, Thomas C. <u>December's Child</u>. University of California Press, 1975.

10. Steven W. Hackel. <u>Children of Coyote, Missionaries of Saint Francis</u>. University of North Carolina Press, 2005.

11. John P. Harrington's field notes from Maria Solares, Fernando Librado and other Native California consultants. Available through the J.P. Harrington Database Project located in the Culture Department of the Pechanga Tribe near Temecula, California.

12. Sherburne F. Cook. <u>The Conflict Between the California Indian and White Civilization</u>. University of California Press, 1976.

About the Author

Gary Robinson, a writer and filmmaker of Choctaw and Cherokee Indian descent, has spent more than twenty-five years working with American Indian communities to tell the historical and contemporary stories of Native peoples in all forms of media.

Much of his recent work has focused on telling the truth about California history with his production of *Telling the Truth about California Missions* and *Tears of our Ancestors: Healing from Historical Trauma*, two educational films available from Tribal Eye Productions

His television work has aired on PBS, FNX Network, Turner Broadcasting, and other networks. Some of his most recent work can be seen online at Native Flix (www.nativeflix.com). His non-fiction books, <u>From Warriors to Soldiers</u> and <u>The Language of Victory</u>, have revealed little-known apsects of American Indian service in the U.S. military from the Revolutionary War to modern times.

He is also the author of several teen novels in the *PathFinders* series published by 7th Generation/Native Voices Books. This unique series features Native American teen main characters who go on adventures and rediscover the value of their own tribal identities. (www.NativeVoicesBooks.com)

His children's books include <u>Native American Night Before Christmas</u> and <u>Native American Twelve Days of Christmas</u>, published by Clearlight Books of Santa Fe.

All his books are available on Amazon.com.

He lives in rural central California. More information about the author can be found at www.tribaleyeproductions.com and www.youtube. com/tribaleyepro. Like his Facebook page: facebook.com/tribaleyepro.

CPSIA information can be obtained
at www.ICGtesting.com
Printed in the USA
LVHW020210080820
662602LV00015B/632